The Boy
with
Paper Wings

Susan Lowell

Illustrations by Paul Mirocha

Paper Engineering by Rhod Lauffer

MILKWEED
EDITIONS

©1995, Text by Susan Lowell
©1995, Cover and interior illustrations by Paul Mirocha. Paper engineering by Rhod Lauffer. Illustrations © 1995 Paul Mirocha and Rhod Lauffer.
All rights reserved. Except for brief quotations in critical articles or reviews, no part of this book may be reproduced in any manner without prior written permission from the publisher: Milkweed Editions, 430 First Avenue North, Suite 400, Minneapolis, MN 55401
Distributed by Publishers Group West

Published 1995 by Milkweed Editions
Printed in the United States of America
Book design by Will Powers.
The text of this book is set in ITC Stone Serif.
                 98 99   5 4 3
First Edition

Milkweed Editions is a not-for-profit publisher. We gratefully acknowledge support from Target Stores, Dayton's, and Mervyn's by the Dayton Hudson Foundation; Ecolab Foundation; General Mills Foundation; Honeywell Foundation; Jerome Foundation; John S. and James L. Knight Foundation; The McKnight Foundation; Andrew W. Mellon Foundation; Minnesota State Arts Board through an appropriation by the Minnesota State Legislature; Challenge and Literature Programs of the National Endowment for the Arts; I. A. O'Shaughnessy Foundation; Piper Jaffray Companies, Inc.; John and Beverly Rollwagen Fund of the Minneapolis Foundation; The St. Paul Companies, Inc.; Star Tribune/Cowles Media Foundation; Surdna Foundation; James R. Thorpe Foundation; Lila Wallace-Reader's Digest Literary Publishers Marketing Development Program, funded through a grant to the Council of Literary Magazines and Presses; and generous individuals.

Library of Congress Cataloging-in-Publication Data

Lowell, Susan, 1950–
     The boy with paper wings / Susan Lowell ; illustrations by Paul
Mirocha. — 1st ed.
        p. cm.
     Summary: When a fever confines eleven-year-old Paul to bed, he folds paper to create imaginary playmates and to transport himself into other worlds. Includes instructions for paper folding.
     ISBN 1-57131-008-8 (Cloth). — ISBN 1-57131-604-3 (pbk.)
     [1. Sick—Fiction. 2. Paper work—Fiction. 3. Handicraft—Fiction.
4. Imaginary playmates—Fiction.] I. Mirocha, Paul, ill. II. Title.
PZ7.L9648Bo   1995
[Fic]—dc20   95-12818
                                                       CIP
                                                        AC

This book is printed on acid-free paper.

To Anne, Rick, Katie, and Paul

For their technical advice and assistance, and their inspiration, I owe many thanks to Paul and Rick Wallat, David Gay, Paul Mirocha, Rhod Lauffer, and Scott Elliott. I am also very grateful to Max Hulme and Nick Robinson for generously giving me permission to reproduce Mr. Hulme's airplane design in this book.

The Boy with Paper Wings

Index of Paper-Folding Projects

I saw a Line that was no Line; Space that was not Space: I was myself, and not myself. When I could find voice, I shrieked aloud in agony, "Either this is madness or it is Hell." "It is neither," calmly replied the voice of the Sphere, "It is Knowledge; it is Three Dimensions: open your eye once again and try to look steadily."

I looked, and, behold, a new world!

—Edwin A. Abbott, *Flatland: A Romance of Many Dimensions*

The Boy with Paper Wings

Home

Paul lay flat on his back
in bed with a fever.
    In a sky like blue paint,
the sun burned brightly, but Paul had the shivers.
His teeth almost chewed up the thermometer.
    "No school for you," said his mother, pulling up
the blanket.
    "Yes!" thought Paul happily, and he began to
make wonderful plans. First, he would launch all his
model rockets. And then he would build a fine new
periscope tower to top off his tree fort. After that, he
would improve the wolf snare that guarded the foot
of his ladder, and then . . .
    "Lie still," Mom said, studying the thermometer.
    At last she gave the little silvery wand a quick
shake, and then, to Paul's horror, she announced:
"You'll have to stay in bed."
    "Oh, no!" he groaned.
    A long boring day stretched ahead of him like
a blank page. How would he ever fill it?
    For Paul was a boy who never did nothing. His

thoughts jumped from his head to his hands and then out of his fingertips in the shape of drawings, models, structures, machines, and, occasionally, big trouble. For example, there was the time he built a really excellent stink bomb and exploded it beneath his younger sister Katie's bed . . .

This morning, more than usual, he wished he could fly out the window and escape. Like a blue ski slope, the wide-open sky seemed to cry out to him: "Try me!" Often, often, Paul dreamed of flying.

"But not like Peter Pan," he thought scornfully.

He, Paul, would die before he let anybody catch *him* in clothes as dumb as Peter Pan's. Tights! And a little green skirt! What a total dweeb, like some disgusting thing that you might see if you got dragged to your sister's ballet recital!

"I'd throw it all away, except the sword," thought Paul, who preferred to wear powerful, mysterious black clothes, or else military camouflage.

He knew that fairy dust would never make him fly. Fairy dust was just as ridiculous as Tinker Bell's feeble little wings, which wouldn't even hold up a mosquito, let alone some ding-a-ling in a tutu. And speaking of feeble, what about Icarus? How dumb could you be, if your wings were made of feathers and wax, to fly so near the sun? No wonder he crashed! But Paul was quite sure that if he put his own mind to the job, he could imagine, design, and build some way for a real boy to fly.

Imagination was the beginning of it all. By taking a deep breath and concentrating hard, Paul could create the feeling of flight. He rose from the bed, his stomach swirled with excitement, his arms and legs grew light, the wind washed his hair and combed his fingers, and he swam through the air as though it were dry water. He weighed less than a soap bubble. He soared higher than a bird, higher than a rocket . . .

For an instant this was all real; then the magic evaporated. Poof! Thump!

Paul found himself flat on his back again. If only his head didn't feel so strange! And if only he didn't have to stay in bed!

"Aw, *fishcakes!*" he said, using an expression he'd just invented, but unfortunately it had no effect on Mom.

"You may read, and you may play quiet games," she said, "but no running around! Not till your temperature goes down. And no TV! You watched so much yesterday that I'm surprised you still have a brain in your head."

She looked down at him with a worry mark between her eyebrows.

"We have to take care of that brain," she said softly.

"Why did this have to happen to me?" grumbled Paul.

"You're sick," said his mother. "It's probably some kind of virus, and your body is trying to

Home   3

burn it up with fever and demolish it with antibodies. Your job is to help win the battle."

She smoothed his dark wispy hair back from his forehead with her cool fingertips.

"I've got to go to work, Paul," she said finally. "But Dad will be right in the next room. Get well, now!"

She blew him a kiss from the doorway, and then her heels went clack-clack down the hall and out of the house. Through the stillness that followed, Paul heard the distant voice of his father's computer, humming and clicking and sometimes giving a small electronic toot. Katie had already gone to school, so now he and his father, who worked at home, were the only people left in the house.

What to do? Paul's strange shivers had stopped, leaving him drained of all his usual energy. His feet seemed too heavy to move, and his elbows ached. So he sank back against his pillow, and as he lay there in the silence, he began to hear a sound that was low and far away and monotonous, but very terrible.

Na na na. Na na na na.

It was a secret that he had never told anyone — something truly frightening that happened inside his head occasionally when he had a fever. He called it the Voice.

Na na na.

That was all it ever said. Over and over. It didn't scream or explode or hypnotize him with a bright flicker, like TV, but the quiet drone of *na na na* tried to take control of all his other thoughts, and that was very scary. If he wasn't careful, the pattern on his wallpaper would start to throb in time with the *na-na* rhythm. There was only one way to fight the fever Voice, besides getting well, and that was to drown it out with different thoughts. Rapid motion also helped. He must *do* something!

Paul shook his head hard. This seemed to stop the sinister Voice — for now at least — so he relaxed, gazing out the window again at the blue-paint sky.

A row of purple mountains covered the bottom of his view. High above them, one small frizzy cloud reminded Paul of the cotton ball that his mother had pulled from the top of the pill bottle before she gave him his medicine. Half a moon hung beside the cloud, and as Paul sat there, watching, watching, a tiny silver airplane crept slowly across the sky.

A great idea zoomed into Paul's head.

Not long ago, for his eleventh birthday, his parents had given him a big box of craft supplies. Since his shelves and his closet were already overflowing with equipment and inventions, he'd stashed the birthday box underneath his bed.

He dangled his upper body over the edge of the mattress.

Home

"Watch out!" he warned himself.

Forgetting about the Voice, Paul pretended that the bed was a raft floating across a sea full of monsters. Unless he was extremely quick, something with terrible fish fangs, sharper than butcher knives, stronger than pruning shears, might just snap his arm off at the elbow —

Whew! He was safe. He dragged the box onto the raft and peered inside. Glue, clay, balsa wood . . .

"No," thought Paul. "Paper."

He fingered the different sheets thoughtfully: new, recycled, colored, lined, patterned, heavy, light, crisp, soft, shiny, rough, transparent . . . Paper was great stuff, Paul thought. You could do almost anything with it.

Today he would make a paper airplane. *He* might have to stay in bed, but at least *it* could fly, and he would imagine himself as the pilot.

But what kind of airplane?

"Not just any old paper airplane," Paul decided. Somewhere lately he had seen a simple but quite special plane, a stunt plane. Yes! Now he remembered how to fold it.

Paul chose a square of yellow-and-white origami paper and laid it flat, with the yellow side down. He folded it neatly in half, and then in half again to mark its exact center.

Then he opened the sheet out flat again and doubled up the bottom quarter to match the central crease.

He folded a triangle in each lower corner, and folded the bottom corners to the center line, beginning the wings.

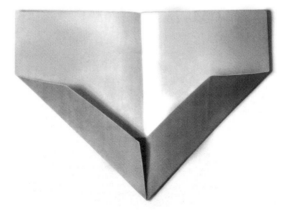

Next he creased the sharp tip neatly in half and bent it underneath until the point met the exact center of the paper. Now the plane had a snub nose, but its wings weren't complete.

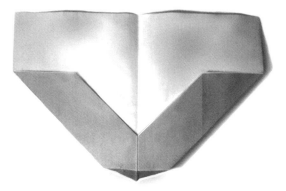

So Paul folded it precisely in half, like a butterfly at rest, and then he folded each half in half again, lining up all the edges.

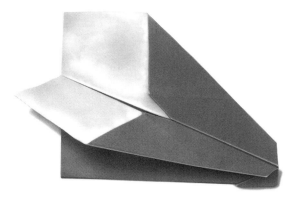

After opening it up, he added an important finishing touch: using his fingernails, he curled each wing tip slightly upward. (These odd little curves were necessary to make the airplane fly well.) And now the plane was done.

War

Paul paused for a moment
to admire his new creation.
"I hereby name you . . .
Yes! . . . *Sky Slicer,*" he said aloud.
He imagined himself zipping his flight suit,
adjusting his helmet, and climbing on board. He
buckled his seat belt and seized the controls.

Then he raised his arm, bent his elbow, drew a
deep breath, and launched the Sky Slicer high into
the air above his bed. The airplane climbed steeply
toward the ceiling, which Paul had decorated with
glow-in-the-dark stars and planets. The plane soared
silently among the airless galaxies. Then, pursued
by ravenous aliens, it headed right for a black
hole . . .

Uh-oh! Mayday! Help! The Slicer bounced off the
Big Dipper and whirled dizzily down again to land
on Paul's pillow.

At that moment Paul's young black cat, Scout,
poked his head into the open doorway, and Paul sat
up and called to him. Scout hesitated, amazed to

find Paul in bed at this time of day, but after a moment he padded into the bedroom, blinking his mint-green eyes and switching his long tail from side to side.

"Look, Scout," Paul said. He launched the Sky Slicer again, this time holding it upside down, just to see if it would also fly with the wings on top.

It did. It whipped around in a big loop that grazed the pointed tips of Scout's ears.

"Yow! Yizz!" squawked the cat. He batted the plane out of the air and bolted down the hall with every hair on his tail electrified by fright.

"Scout! I didn't mean to! It was an accident. Come back!"

But Scout did not.

"Dang!" said Paul. Quickly he slipped out of bed and retrieved the plane, jumping back under the covers again before the hammerheads and barracudas could catch a whiff of his bare toes. The Sky Slicer had suffered serious damage in the attack. In fact, it was shredded.

"Now what?" Paul wondered.

The door of Paul's closet stood ajar, like the mouth of a cave. It was a fine target, he decided, but to penetrate the dark he needed a new plane, a night-flier, tricky to fold but silent in the air . . .

He began with a plain white square. Fold by fold, the night bird took shape, and when it was done Paul named it the Owl.

Its pilot must wear night-vision goggles: owl eyes for seeing in the dark. When they were properly set upon his head, he taxied down the runway, revved the engines, and took off.

He aimed the Owl over the perilous ocean. It glided below the stars this time . . . past Paul's hanging model of the Space Shuttle ("Keep your needles centered," Paul told himself as he checked his instruments) . . . past the checkered wing of a woodpecker (one of Scout's victims) that Paul had mounted on his wall . . . and then down, down, down, neatly, silently through the closet door ("Yay!" breathed Paul), and into the cave, and . . . click.

Click. Click.

What was that tiny sound? Paul hopped out of bed again and went to investigate. Perhaps, he thought, the airplane had accidentally hit a switch on one of his many inventions. Flinging open the closet door, he confronted the jumble of objects inside, very few of which were clothes.

Paul inspected his various machines, but none of them were clicking. His catapult sat perfectly still, his hovercraft lay belly-up, and his Mars-mobile was missing its motor and wheels, which he had stolen for another project. His model boats were all in dry dock.

Lower down in the closet, a bizarre little figure sat perched on the edge of a shelf with its bottom half dangling into space. Its body was sculpted from green and blue modeling clay, and although it had legs and arms (one was a machine gun), it lacked feet and hands. Its head was a small army tank, and bits of armor were positioned here and there across its body, like irregular fish scales. A pair of gun barrels sprouted from its shoulders, and it wore what seemed to be a transparent air bottle on its back. A gun turret projected from the middle of its face, but since it had neither eyes nor mouth, you could never say it stared back at you.

The figure was part of a new, top-secret fantasy project of Paul's, but he still had his doubts about this particular sculpture. Was it a superhero, or was it an archenemy? Although Paul hadn't quite finished it yet, something about the model bothered him. He thought he might have to knead it down to clay again, and start over.

Click. Click. Click.

Anyway, how could that creature click? It had no moving parts.

Then Paul looked down at the floor and saw that the Owl had crashed in the middle of a war. It lay, a crumpled wreck, among the tiny soldiers of a military diorama on the closet floor. In order to see better, Paul got down on his stomach.

Amidst sandy hills and valleys, a silver stripe of river, and many miniature trees, one army, painted green, was in the act of ambushing another, painted gray. Puffs of cotton smoke erupted from their guns. Pools of red paint flowed from their wounds. A road sign was riddled with bullet holes that Paul had made with a hot needle stuck in a cork; the Styrofoam bridge over the river had been partly demolished by a candle flame, or possibly grenades.

He laid his head sideways on the cool, gritty floor and began to think himself into the scene. It was easy to imagine living in the closet, especially if it were a cave, and if he were smaller . . .

"There's so much more room when you shrink," he thought dreamily.

Click. No, it wasn't a click. It was — *ping!* Something hard sang across the top of Paul's head, ruffling his hair. It was gunfire! And it was followed by an explosion that shook the floor beneath Paul's body. Covering his ears, he felt an icy pang of true fear.

"Bad guys must have gotten into the house!" he thought.

Where was Dad? Somehow Paul must warn him. In the meantime he must take cover. But where? He couldn't see his bed anymore, just piles of rubble, and the bomb must have blown out one of the walls of his bedroom, for he could feel a chilly wind blowing, and he could see the blue sky overhead, clouded with several of the frizzy cotton balls that he remembered from earlier that morning, only now they reminded him more of smoke. The half moon had moved a little farther down the sky.

Ping!

"Dang!" Paul dove behind the nearest tree, his heart pounding. Luckily he was wearing his camouflage pajamas.

"Hey, buddy," called a man's voice.

Paul opened his mouth to answer, and then he froze. Who were the good guys, anyway? Which side was he on? He looked down frantically at his pajamas. The camouflage pattern contained both green and gray, and some brown, too. Maybe they were a little more green than gray; it was hard to decide.

"Help me," pleaded the voice, which now seemed to come from the branches above Paul's head. Then the leaves parted, and halfway up the tree Paul saw a face not much older than his own, yet old enough to grow a dark stubble of unshaved whiskers from his wax-pale skin. To Paul's relief, the soldier also wore greenish camouflage, including a helmet disguised with netting and leaves. But then the boy noticed that one sleeve of the man's uniform was soaked with a dark sticky substance. It was not red paint.

"Oh — my — gosh," he thought, feeling sick. "It's real blood."

The soldier spoke again. "Can you get me a bandage?"

In a daze, Paul found a length of strange glittering lavender cloth lying almost underneath his feet. He tore a strip from it and helped the young man tie it around his wounded shoulder.

"Thanks," he said, leaning back exhausted when they were done.

Luckily, the bandage seemed to stop the bleeding, and Paul's stomach no longer felt queasy.

"I'm Paul," he ventured.

"Joe," said the soldier.

"Can you tell me . . . " Paul asked nervously, "what's going on?"

"Braindrainers," said Joe. "Tried to break through the pass. But we nailed 'em pretty good. I hope we did, anyway. When *this* happened, I had to stay behind."

More shots rang out, and the soldier raised a finger to his lips.

War   17

"What are Braindrainers?" whispered Paul.

"Why are you asking all these questions?" Joe hissed, suddenly tense. "Where's your gun? Are you a Green or a Drainer?"

"I — I'm not a soldier at all."

Joe narrowed his eyes. "That makes no difference. To me or to *them.*"

He pulled his own gun into his lap and aimed it at Paul.

"No! Please! I'll help you if I can," Paul cried. "But I still don't understand."

After studying him carefully, Joe lowered his weapon. "Well," he said at last, "it seems like your brain is still in your head, but it's working awful slow. Listen, kid. Our job is to stop the Drainers. Nothing else matters."

"You mean," gasped Paul, "they — they'll take our brains away?"

"Suck 'em dry."

"How?"

"Micropumps," said Joe. "Sssssllp! Right out the ear."

"*Why?*"

"To take 'em back to KRON. The Drainers work for KRON. KRON is their Commander. Don't you know *anything?*"

Paul shook his head wonderingly. "It's like a dream. It's like I just landed here."

"Say!" exclaimed Joe. "Just before I got hit, a plane crashed. No pilot. Seemed to be a white drone. We thought it must be some kind of enemy brainplane, but it sure made a lucky landing for our side. Killed a bunch of Drainers. Maybe you were the pilot and hit your head in the crash."

Paul put his hands up to his skull and felt it cautiously; there were no lumps, but he was still confused. Nevertheless, he told himself, he must fight the Braindrainers, and he must find his father.

"Joe?"

"What?" snapped Joe, whose attention seemed distracted.

"Who's KRON?"

"Shh! I think I hear Drainers. Climb the tree quick, get out of sight, and shut up."

War

KRON

Desperately clinging to the
harsh tree trunk, hoping
that the leaves would screen
him from the Braindrainers, Paul held his breath
and waited. At least Joe's gun was cocked and ready,
and Paul had found a good vantage point, even if he
didn't know what the heck he was looking for.

It fell, finally, right out of the sky above Paul's
head. Did it fall from an airplane, or off a cliff? Did it
simply materialize out of thin air? He could not tell.

It landed in a small clearing not far from Joe and
Paul's tree, with a hideous thud that rattled their
bones. They froze. After lying still for a few seconds,
as though stunned, it gathered itself up, mashed all
its broken bits together again, and rose slowly to its
stumps, uglier than ever, an appalling, monstrous
lump of clay and weaponry, without eyes, ears, fingers, or toes. Danger radiated from it like a bad smell.

Paul stared in horrified fascination. He recognized it.

It was his own sculpture, come dreadfully to life.

He watched as it crept off through the woods —
stump, stomp, stump, stomp — moving, fortunately, in the opposite direction from the tree where
the two camouflaged figures hid. And it was lucky
also, Paul thought, that the grisly tank-head could
not turn. He knew without being told that now
this thing had a life of its own. It was no longer his
creation, but his enemy, and everyone else's enemy,
too. He wished with all his heart that he had never
made it.

Its appearance triggered other memories as well.
Something tugged at the corner of his mind, something evil and disturbing, and yet also very familiar.
What was it? Paul struggled to remember, but it
remained out of reach, like a tune he couldn't quite
recall. It was almost as if the creature were talking to
him, and the message was unintelligible but still
frightening. Then it came to him: *Na na na na.* It
was calling to him in the Voice!

When at last the clay figure had completely disappeared, Joe leaned forward and spat upon the
ground.

"KRON," he said. It sounded like a curse.

"I thought it was a Drainer," whispered Paul.

Joe shook his head grimly.

"That's KRON itself. It steals brains and implants
them wherever it wants," he said. "It keeps its own
brain in its belly, which is the central control. That's
how it can have a tank for a head. It's building some
kind of worldwide computer network, too. But it

also implants the brains in machines . . . killer-crawlers, deathdiggers, lifecrushers, smartbombs. It's a virus, sort of like a life form, only it's a death form instead. Like AIDS. Like cancer. Only bigger, because it wants total control. Do you get it now, kid? KRON has to be wiped out. But how?"

Joe paused and leaned back in despair. "You saw how it repaired itself just now."

"No wonder it gave me a bad feeling!" said Paul, thinking of the figure he had placed on the edge of the closet shelf.

"Bad!" snorted Joe. "KRON is worse than bad."

"But I don't understand. How do these things happen? Where did it get that name? Why now? Why me? What should I do?"

"You ask too many questions, kid," said Joe. "All I know is, it's KRON or us. Simple as that."

To give himself time and space to think about these problems, Paul shinnied away from Joe to the top of the tree, and there he made a great discovery.

"Hey, I know where we are!" he cried.

The river valley surrounded by hills that lay spread out below him was the very landscape that he himself had painstakingly created, molding the shapes from clay, gluing real sand and rocks to them, and painting in the details with tiny brushes. Paul loved details; the more he added, the more real his little worlds became.

"But I never imagined anything *this* real," he thought, awestruck.

KRON

Paul even recognized some of his own model- and machine-building equipment lying scattered among the trees at the edge of the woods — his tweezers, his tiny pliers, his tubes of special glue, his spools of wire and string — as well as a few matches and two or three precious, perilous firecrackers.

"Gee, I thought I cleaned up," he said to himself. "I'd better put that stuff away before Mom gets home."

Although his mother had a strong prejudice against any kind of fire in his bedroom, Paul always kept a secret stash of matches there.

Paul also realized, with a shock, that the dreaded Braindrainers must be the little soldiers that he personally had painted gray. He knew that underneath the paint they were just as green as the others; he had bought them all together in a bag. This thought made him feel confused and sad, but there was no time to worry about it now.

Ping! Ping! Boom! From the treetop he could see that the battle continued to rage in the pass, but now the green defenders were falling back and gray reinforcements were streaming down to join the attacking army. Something must be done, and fast! Paul scanned the woods, but KRON himself was nowhere to be seen.

Just then Paul noticed a large object that he didn't recognize, a long, narrow shape, half pink and half lavender, partly hidden from view by clumps of what appeared to be unraveled rope, or perhaps dry grass. What could it be? Surely it had nothing to do with KRON. At least it lay perfectly still; perhaps it was dead, or . . . drained. Shuddering with disgust, Paul glanced back at the battle, and then an idea struck him.

"Joe," he called down softly. "I think I know how we can stop the Drainers."

"How?" said Joe skeptically.

"Well, there's a small, deep valley behind the pass," said Paul.

"What of it?"

"There's another pass at the end of the valley, and beyond it the mountains. I know the geography. What if our men fell back into the mountains, trapped 'em in the valley, and blew 'em all to smithereens?"

"Yeah, right. Great idea," said Joe sarcastically. "Where do we get a big enough bomb? And what about KRON?"

"Well," said Paul, "I could make a bomb."

"A kid like you? Out of what? Bubble gum?"

Paul had just finished explaining his plan, which Joe admitted just might work, when a squeaky little voice interrupted them.

KRON

Barbie

"Guys? Oh, *guys?*" it called.

Joe gave a start. "What's that?"

Paul saw a slight upheaval in the mysterious clumps of dry grass.

"Yoo hoo!" yodeled the voice.

"Freeze!" bellowed Joe, waving his gun.

"I already *am*," said the voice, turning into a whine. "Flat on my face for *hours!* My clothes are a mess, and my *hair's* going to need some *serious* work. First, there was that *panther.* He's like sniff-sniff and I'm like oh, gross, eat me up why don't you and get it *over* with? Then *he* left, and that *other* thing came, and he's like stump-stomp and I'm like totally petrified out of my *mind,* but he left, too."

A flat, unblinking turquoise eye appeared through the shredded fibers.

"Barbie!" cried Paul. "What are you doing here?"

Her pink mouth smiled, but Barbie continued to whine. "Katie dropped me," she complained. "She was snooping in your closet and *she* left me behind, *too.* Everybody leaves me. Nobody wants me. Can you believe it? Can you *imagine* what that does to my self-esteem? A girl like me?"

"What panther?" said Joe.

"The *black* kind, dummy," said Barbie impatiently.

"KRON must have passed her by!" marveled Paul.

Barbie squealed louder than ever. "I've been stuck in this dump for *days,* and these war games are getting me *down,* and I want to go home to my yacht and my dream house and my beauty parlor *now.*"

"Well, why don't you just get up and go?" said Joe.

"*I* can't walk," wailed Barbie. "I can move my joints, but that's all. How *could* I walk on these feet?"

She kicked her tiny bent stubs helplessly in the air. She had lost her high-heeled slippers, and she was dressed in a pink bathing suit, a glittering lavender tutu, and a gold plastic crown.

"We don't have time to help you," said Joe. "This isn't a game, it's real."

To get a better look at him, Barbie rotated her small head on the end of her incredibly long neck, and immediately let out a piercing scream. "You're wearing my *scarf!* You got *blood* on it! Yuck!"

"Get your boyfriend to rescue you," Paul suggested. "What's his name? The boy Barbie? He has flat feet, hasn't he?"

"Ken? That wimp! He's *never* there when I want

him. He's always out with some *other* Barbie, and then he *says* he can't tell us apart. Ken's like a total airhead!"

"Well," said Paul, as he helped Joe climb down from the tree, "I'm sorry, Barbie, but we have to go fight a battle now."

Her long skinny legs drummed up and down in a tantrum.

"No! No! Don't leave me alone! I'm afraid of the panther, and I'm *dying* to change these clothes."

As Paul stood there staring at her, another idea suddenly occurred to him. "Let's take her with us," he said to Joe.

"Are you serious? She'll wreck everything."

"I think she can help us," said Paul. He knelt beside Barbie. "Listen," he told her, nose to nose. "This is your only chance. If KRON and the Braindrainers win the war, they'll take your yacht and your sports car and your castle and implant brains in them and make them do bad work for KRON. They *might* even put brains in *you!*"

"WAAAA," bawled Barbie.

"But if you help us, we'll save the world, and you can go back to Katie's room and everything will be just the way it was before."

"Oh, all *right,*" she sniffled.

"How are we going to move her?" objected Joe. "She's taller than a telephone pole."

"I know," said Paul, grinning. "But she does have a handle."

Barbie   *29*

Ignoring Barbie's protests, they dragged her gently through the woods by her hair. Fortunately, being plastic, she was not heavy and did not feel pain, and she quieted down when Paul told her that screams attracted panthers. He couldn't imagine where she had gotten the panther idea; he himself was mostly afraid of KRON. When they got close to the battleground, they stopped and covered Barbie with leaves while Paul and Joe reconnoitered. Paul quickly found the firecrackers, wires, matches, fuses, ropes, and everything else he needed to build the bomb, so he sat down under a tree and went to work.

Just beyond the pass, down in the little valley, they could hear the gruesome sound of fighting.

Zing! Ping!

"Aaaaah!"

"Hurry!" said Joe.

"I wish I could test it first," said Paul, "but this will have to do."

"Are you sure you can launch it by yourself?" asked Joe.

"No problem," said Paul, sounding more certain than he really felt, because with bombs, you never quite knew what might happen. "Go and warn the Greens," he went on, "and remember to give me the signal as soon as the Drainers take control of the valley."

Joe hesitated for a moment, looking doubtful. "I hate to leave you here alone, kid," he said.

"I'm okay," said Paul. "It's all my fault, really, so I have to help."

"Your fault?"

"Yes. I — I made KRON."

"*You* made KRON?" said Joe incredulously. "You're joking. You must be lightheaded!"

"I just don't understand how it got so big, and went so bad."

Joe shook his head in obvious disbelief, pushing all these thoughts aside. "It doesn't matter now. Look, kid, I have to keep the gun, but I'm going to give you my survival knife, just in case."

"Oh, wow!" said Paul.

The knife was forged from the finest steel and inlaid with a single crimson flame made of some substance that sent out sparks like a jewel. With all of its blades and attachments folded up, the survival knife exactly fitted inside his right palm, as though it had been made to measure for him. Paul closed his fingers around the knife with joy. It was just what he'd always wanted.

Joe raised his good arm in a quick salute, and melted into the bushes without another word. Walking very carefully, Paul carried the bomb back to the pile of leaves and hair. Now, he thought, everything would depend on Barbie, and he hoped he could persuade her to play her part.

"Where have you *been?* I am beautiful and glamorous and sick and tired of being left behind and

Barbie

31

treated this way and I've got twigs in my teeth and *ants* in my *tutu!* I quit!"

"Barbie," said Paul in a very serious tone, "you are going to be a hero."

"Why should I be a hero?" she squeaked. "I'm *already* famous. Look at my *crown. I* am a *princess!"*

"You can lift your arms, right?" said Paul, ignoring her proclamations.

As soon as she did, he quickly tied a rope around her.

"Stop it! That tickles!"

"After this, they'll call you Mighty Power Barbie or something," he promised, rigging up a pulley over a tree branch. "Won't that be great?"

"What will the clothes be like?" she asked suspiciously.

"Bulletproof," said Paul.

He began to raise her to a standing position, which was tricky because her odd shrunken feet were almost useless for balance.

"Eeeee!"

She wobbled in dizzy circles, gradually rising until she was the tallest object in the vicinity, even higher than the hill that lay between them and the battle. Her little blonde head must be visible from the valley, Paul guessed, and he hastily lowered her down again.

"Luckily, we already know that KRON has no interest in her," he thought.

So far, no signal had come from Joe.

"Okay, Barbie. Take this."

"What *is* it?" she wanted to know.

"A bomb. Don't drop it."

"Eeeee! Take it back! I told you I don't *want* to be a hero!"

"You have to," Paul told her. "You're the only one who can. You have the height and the leverage. Shhh!"

He clamped his hand over her smiling pink mouth, for the sounds of fighting had dropped off. He listened intently, and sure enough he heard Joe's signal: two short, sharp whistles followed by one long one. The Greens must have retreated into the mountains, leaving the Drainers in the valley.

"Barbie," he whispered. "I'm going to pull you up again so that you face away from the hill. I know you can't throw forwards because your arms don't work that way, so we're doing this backwards. Wait till I say, "Now," and then throw the bomb as hard as you can, over your head and into the valley. Okay? Please?"

He took his hand off her mouth, and for a long moment she was silent. Suddenly Paul felt sorry for her. Poor Barbie, he thought. She'd never asked to be involved in any of this. What right had he to make her into a bomber? Why, he was acting just as bad as KRON!

Then she murmured thoughtfully, "Mighty *Power* Barbie? Me?"

"Yes," said Paul solemnly. "This will make you

Barbie

different from all other Barbies, forever. But listen, Barbie, you don't have to do it if you don't want to. I'll figure out some other way, a giant slingshot maybe — "

But she interrupted him.

"What're you *waiting* for?" said Barbie. "Pull the rope. Let's go go *go!*"

"Now," he said, an instant later.

"Cowabunga!" screamed Barbie.

And just as she hurled the bomb, the panther pounced.

Flight

For an instant after the
explosion (but how long
all of this lasted Paul never
really knew) everything went black. Then Paul
found himself lying at the bottom of his closet
with toys scattered all around him and Scout sitting
on his face. The charred, rotten-egg smell of gun-
powder smoke filled his bedroom. Paul felt groggy,
as well as cold from lying on the floor, and, to his
great dismay, deep inside his head the Voice was
droning again: *na na na na*. His fingers stung from
a slight burn, and there was also a sharp pain in his
palm.

Yowling, Scout leaped from Paul's head to the
bed, and then to the bedside table, where he
knocked over Paul's water glass, which immediately
smashed into a hundred pieces.

"Krr-ow!" cried the cat wildly.

He vaulted over the puddle of water and broken
glass and whisked out the door, almost colliding
with Paul's father.

"What happened?" Dad exclaimed.

Cautiously Paul sat up, and the Voice faded away. Then he looked with dazed eyes at the mess all around him. What *had* happened? Had they stopped the invasion of Drainers? Where had everybody gone?

"Oh, Dad," he said. "I meant to warn you — "

His father bent down and laid a hand on Paul's forehead. "Are you all right?" he said. "You certainly feel hot."

"I do feel kind of weird," said Paul. His skin seemed to be twinkling, and Dad looked small and far away, although not nearly as small as the soldiers in his army scene, or the Barbie doll that lay beside it.

"Your hand is bleeding," said Dad.

"Not much." Paul gazed at the red marks on his palm, which might be cat scratches or might — just might — be caused by something else.

"What have you done to Katie's doll?"

Poor Barbie! She had gone to pieces. Her arms were tangled up in a piece of string, and somehow she had lost her head, her crown, and one of her legs.

"I'll put her back together again," said Paul guiltily.

"I thought we told you no more bombs."

"It was sort of an accident, Dad," pleaded Paul. "Really. I'm sorry. Things got out of control. And then Scout broke the glass."

He waited for the scolding to begin, but Dad just shook his head wearily as he picked up the largest fragments of glass. "I've never known a clumsier cat," he remarked. "Stay right there, Paul. I don't want you walking around here with bare feet."

He went off to find a broom and a mop.

"I'm sorry," Paul whispered to Barbie, popping the little hollow hairy ball back onto the skinny plastic neck. "You *were* mighty."

Somewhat bedraggled, Barbie smiled but made no answer, and Paul turned to the army diorama.

"Joe?" he called softly. "Can you hear me?"

Within the model world, everything was silent. The tiny trees stood as still as the sandy hills, the painted river, and the miniature soldiers, gray and green. But wait! Paul caught his breath, and pushed his face down closer, his eyes widening as he noticed that most of the gray soldiers lay flat on their faces in the valley, while the Greens hid by twos and threes among the mountains. He could not tell which one, if any, wore a lavender bandage on his arm.

Where, he wondered next with a flash of panic, was KRON? A quick search of the closet revealed no trace of the ugly clay figure.

"Did it get away?" Paul thought. "Oh, *fishcakes!*"

When he heard his father returning, Paul pushed the diorama into a dark corner. He could never explain all the things that had happened, he realized, so he'd better not try. And also a faint shadow

Flight

of doubt had crossed his mind: when he had touched the soldiers, he had found that they were all glued tightly to the board. *Had* the scene really been different before, or was he remembering it wrong? Now he felt completely puzzled.

He stretched out a hand and rescued the crumpled Owl from the edge of the flood and thoughtfully reshaped its wings and sharpened its folds.

"Dad," said Paul, "why can a piece of paper fly, but not me?"

Once again he thought that if any boy should be able to fly, he was the one. He was not too big, he was not at all fat, he was very wiry and strong, and his desire was so strong!

Dad closed his eyes and puckered his face into a thinking expression that made Paul laugh, and then after a moment an answer rumbled out of his beard: "PHYSICS."

"Dad!" cried Paul reproachfully. "That's not enough. Tell me more."

So his father took a thin strip of paper, held it just below Paul's lower lip, and told him to blow. Paul did: "FFFFfff" went his feverish breath across his lip, and even though he was blowing down on the paper, the drooping strip rose up and floated in the air.

"That is called *lift*," said his father. "The air that you blew across the top of the paper moved faster than the air below the paper. And, believe it or not, a fast stream of air has a lower pressure than a slow one, so the slower, stronger air underneath lifted up the sheet."

"Lift," echoed Paul, blowing again. Lift was what he needed, he thought. Surely if he built himself some sort of wing, the rest would follow.

"I don't want to fly just to *fly*," Paul thought. "I would fly to my friends' houses, so nobody would have to drive me there. I would fly to school. And whenever I liked, I would fly *out* of school!"

Dad swept up the last crumbs of broken glass and motioned Paul back to bed. As he stood up, something that had been caught in his pajamas tumbled to the floor. It was the survival knife.

Paul gasped and quickly looked at Dad to see if he had noticed, but his father was still happily discussing physics. Paul slipped the knife into his sleeve and obediently climbed between the covers of his bed, his heart thumping so loudly that he could barely hear what his father was saying.

"Lift is one of the forces that helps airplanes fly," Dad went on. "And the angle of the wings, in a V-shape, also helps . . . "

"So everything was real after all!" Paul thought, fingering the knife under the blanket. Little chills rippled up and down his spine; he could hardly contain his excitement. How could he get back there to find out what happened? He put the survival knife back into his sleeve for safekeeping.

Flight

"And then there is *thrust*. Look!" said his father.
Dad took the Owl and threw it in a low, wide curve.

"I provided the thrust for this plane," he said.
"In a big plane or rocket, the engine would."

"But — but — " objected Paul, jiggling the mattress in his impatience. Why couldn't he use the strength of his body for thrust? If he, Paul, had somehow turned the paper Owl into an actual warplane in an actual war, why couldn't he do anything he wanted?

But Dad held up his finger to say "Just wait," and continued. "Each of those forces has an opponent, an enemy. The opposite of thrust is *drag,* everything that sticks out and slows the airplane down."

Paul thought of the way he dragged his feet on the ground when he wanted to stop his bicycle.

"And," his father added, "the opposite of lift is — "

"Gravity!" said Paul. "Crash! Boom! Bang!"

"Exactly," said Dad. He gathered up the mop and the broom. "Gravity is your main enemy, Paul, besides your size and shape. You're a lot bigger than a piece of paper."

"But how do birds and insects fly?" asked Paul, still hopeful.

Very differently from airplanes, his father explained. Natural flight was quite complicated, and it differed from animal to animal. Somewhere Dad had heard that flying through the air feels to a bee the same way that swimming through honey would feel to a person.

Swimming through honey, blue honey, cool, and sticky, and sweet . . . Paul lay back to think it all over while his father took his temperature.

"Good, it's gone down a bit since breakfast," said Dad. "I guess you can't be too sick if you're still able to get in trouble." He skimmed the paper airplane back to Paul. "Don't throw it at Scout," he said.

"I didn't!" protested Paul. "Gosh, Dad! You never know exactly where a paper airplane is going to fly. Sometimes it really surprises you."

"And NO MORE BOMBS!" said Dad. "They destroy property and make a mess, which you must clean up when you're feeling better. And they're dangerous. No more!"

"Okay, I promise," said Paul in a small voice. "But what about war? Don't you have to have bombs in war?"

Dad stroked his beard. It was certainly hard to tell what grown-ups were thinking behind their rocky faces, Paul thought.

At last his father spoke. "Mostly, I agree with Benjamin Franklin, who said there never was a good war, or a bad peace. But we're talking about bombs in your closet, and the main point here is that when you make something, you have to take responsibility for it. And for what it does."

Paul nodded soberly, for he was convinced that no matter what happened, he must try to fly back

Flight

into his adventure. He had a job to do there. The closet door stood open now, and clearly there was no longer a cave inside it, but a different land, far away on the other side of the ocean and beyond the range of the Owl. As soon as his father left the room, Paul selected a fairly heavy sheet of white stationery and began to fold it. For this flight he needed a long-distance, intercontinental flier, an airplane called the Albatross.

Lift," he thought. "Lift! Lift!"

Albatross

The albatross, a mostly
white bird with a big body
and long saber-sharp wings,
glided, and glided, and went on gliding over the
ocean, far above the glittering waves with their endless restless motion, their rough little curls of sea
foam, and their smell of salt and fish and blood.
Peering down over the bird's shoulder, Paul also
glimpsed dark shadows lurking like stains below the
surface of the water. He clung to the albatross's neck
for dear life, and he shivered.

A deep and surprising voice burst from the heavy
beak: "What's the matter?" it asked. "Why do you
shake like that?"

"When a bird makes a noise," Paul thought, "it
should tweet, or maybe screech, or caw. And if it
does talk, it should sound like a parrot, not like a
cross between a bullfrog and a donkey! Where on
earth *am* I?"

Just a moment ago he had been watching his
new plane fly across his bedroom and pretending to

be small enough to ride it, and then a surge of dizziness, or maybe sleepiness, had made him close his eyes, and now . . .

The albatross spoke again. "Are you cold? Are you afraid?"

"Nosy as well as noisy," thought Paul. "But I'd better be polite — it's a long way down!"

He cleared his throat and spoke. "I-it's j-j-j — "

He meant to say that he'd shivered this way earlier that morning because he was sick, not because of cold, or fear. But his teeth clicked together so hard that the words were chopped in bits.

"Pull my feathers over you," brayed the albatross, "and hold on tight."

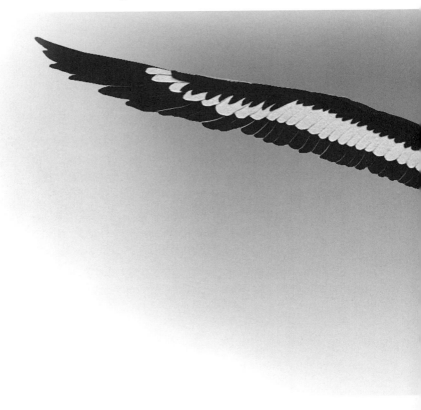

How could a paper bird have feathers? Were they paper feathers? A terrifying thought struck Paul: "Am *I* paper?" When he rubbed his fingers together, they still seemed round, but he himself felt very light — as though his bones were hollow. Then he reached out and felt soft plumage, and as he wriggled deeper into it, he found that it was as warm as his parents' down comforter. This wasn't paper, surely, but real bird feathers.

"Did you molt?" said the albatross, continuing his questions.

"No," said Paul, whose teeth had now stopped chattering. "I'm not a bird. I never had feathers."

He looked down at himself and saw that he was

still wearing his camouflage pajamas. Had he shrunk, Paul wondered, or was the albatross enormous? Compared to the vast ocean, there was no way to tell.

"You aren't a fish, are you?" called the albatross hopefully.

Seabirds ate fish, Paul remembered, and indeed the albatross smelled like an old rancid can of Kitty Kaviar, Scout's favorite food. And that armor-plated beak, ending in a hook, looked strong enough to catch and crunch a whale.

"No, I'm not a fish," he said quickly, "although I *can* swim pretty well. Actually, I'm a boy."

"Is that some kind of bug?" said the bird.

"No!"

The albatross laughed a huge strange laugh, a mixture of neighs, whistles, and puppy-dog barks. It was so loud that Paul wanted to cover his ears, but he needed his hands to hang on.

Paul decided that now it was his turn to ask questions. "Please tell me something," he said to the albatross. "Why do you laugh like that?"

"Because I'm a gooney bird!"

"Oh!" said Paul. He had heard of gooney birds, but he hadn't known that they were the same as albatrosses, and since he always loved to find patterns and make connections, he filed this information away in his memory with satisfaction. "And how did *I* get here?" he asked.

"Hush, boy," laughed the albatross. Between the

chuckles, Paul caught the words "worlds within worlds," and then the bird stopped laughing and fell silent.

"Well, then," said Paul, "tell me something else. Where are we going?"

"I do not ask such questions, and I do not answer them," the albatross boomed severely, and Paul was silenced.

All this while they had been gliding, but suddenly the albatross beat his huge wings, rocking Paul where he lay, and then began another majestic glide. Now Paul really began to enjoy the sensations of flight. The albatross's wings cut the air as cleanly as swords, and the pure blue atmosphere seemed to support them as firmly as water or earth. Clouds drifted past like melting feathers. Paul almost lost his fear of falling.

Far below he glimpsed a fleck floating in the sea, and at the same time he felt the albatross suddenly drop toward it.

"A ship," said the bird. "Let's take a look."

The object grew larger and larger, finally becoming a shabby gray freighter dragging a smudge of smoke and an oil slick behind it to pollute the air and water in its wake. The albatross wheeled and flew low across the deck, which Paul now saw was piled with bundles wrapped in sheets of plastic and lashed tightly to the ship with a network of ropes. Dark figures of men, pin sized, appeared between the bundles and stared upward.

Albatross

Then one raised a stick no bigger than a thorn.

At first Paul thought he heard a clap of thunder, but the albatross knew better. He rose as abruptly as he had dived, avoiding two or three more shots as he climbed to safety. Paul tightened the grip of his hands and knees and squeezed his eyes shut. He could not tell whether the heart he felt beating like a bongo drum was his own or the albatross's.

"I am hunted! I am prey!" Paul thought. "I am a bug!"

Then gradually a beautiful glow of relief spread over the boy. They had escaped! Every simple breath of air was a rare treat.

"But *why?*" asked Paul, after being alive had begun to seem normal again. "Why did they shoot?"

"I've seen that ship before," said the bird. "They are smugglers, thieves, destroyers."

"*Drainers,*" thought Paul, chilled again. Aloud, he asked, "What's in the bundles?"

The albatross seemed reluctant to reply, but finally he said, "It's a big network. Guns, maybe. Sometimes drugs. Poisons. And sometimes — "

He left the sentence hanging unfinished and flapped his wings hard.

"*Brains,*" thought Paul.

"Have you ever heard of — KRON?" he asked.

The albatross let out a wild sound that was not a laugh, and they traveled in silence for many miles before Paul dared to speak again. As they flew he studied the albatross's wings, especially the way they were joined to the stout, ducklike body and the way the bird raised them and bent them.

"The angle of attack," he said to himself, remembering Dad's words. At last he couldn't wait any longer to ask the biggest question of all: "How did you learn to fly?"

"Haw!" honked the bird. "I learned as a chick, of course. It's easy! Why do you ask, boy? Can't you fly?"

"No, I can't," said Paul regretfully. "But I'm trying to learn. I'm — I'm a kind of a chick, you see."

"Well, that explains it," the albatross said. "But you can't learn in midair, you know. You learn in your nesting ground. Where *is* your nesting ground, boy?"

"I don't know," said Paul. "I'm lost. Where's yours?"

"Far, far away," croaked the bird.

Suddenly they soared into what appeared to be a bank of fog. Wet whiteness pressed up against Paul's eyes, and he realized that they were flying through a cloud. Then just as suddenly they swam from the cloud into brilliant sun, which made the sea sparkle and the sky glow like colored glass. Paul grew warm, hot, and hotter. He licked his dry lips and tasted a metallic flavor, as though his mouth were full of pennies.

"I'm thirsty," he said. "Don't you ever get that way?"

Albatross

"Haw-haw!" cried the albatross, with another explosion of laughter. "Not with the whole ocean there to drink!"

"But I can't drink salt water," Paul said, feeling thirstier by the minute.

"I can! I separate the salt and squirt it out my nostrils!"

They flew onward. The sun burned steadily on Paul's right, smoldering like a red-hot coal. Paul thought of ice water in tinkling, frosted glasses. He imagined drinking fountains spouting streams as cool and silver to the mouth as liquid mercury to the eye. In his mind, he gobbled handfuls of snow, gulped raindrops, dunked his face in a mountain stream and guzzled. Just when he thought he could bear his thirst no longer, the albatross abruptly took a nosedive toward the sea.

"No! Please!" cried Paul.

But the bird only croaked back, in his strangest voice yet, "Water — water — everywhere!"

As they continued to plummet, Paul couldn't help screaming, but the only sound that reached his ears was the hiss of the wind across his teeth. It was like a dream scream. The ocean below them looked as cold and hard as dented steel. Then at last he saw that they were headed for a small island, no more than an untidy clump of what appeared to be rocks, patched with white, rising from the bounding waves.

Island

Paul braced himself for the
landing, but when it came
it was quite gentle. Widdle-
waddle plop-plop went the albatross, wobbling from
side to side with his webbed feet on the solid
ground, and — oof! — Paul tumbled off his back.

"This is the place where I was hatched, boy," said
the albatross. "Lovely, isn't it?"

Picking himself up, Paul looked around. The
island appeared to be entirely deserted, and a
strange musty, oniony, rubbery smell hung about it.
The sky overhead was full of thin parallel clouds like
fish bones. There were no trees or even weeds, and
the bare ground was pocked with many small hollows with chalk-white broken eggshells scattered in
and around them. The albatross pointed his wing
tip at one of these hollows.

"My nest," he said with pride. "Haw! There's a
spring behind that hill. I don't drink the water
myself — ugh! too sweet! — but it's the kind of stuff
you like."

"Oh, thank you!" said Paul.

Head to one side, the albatross studied him.

"Tk-tk-tk-tk," the bird clicked disapprovingly. "Boys are very strange, very strange. Are those funny little lumps your wings?"

Then, to Paul's dismay, the albatross began to trot and flap his own huge wings in preparation for takeoff. Paul ran along beside him. "Don't go!" he said. "Teach me how to fly!"

But the albatross was already airborne.

"First, make short flights," he chortled. "Then longer. You'll get the hang of it in no time. Haw! Ho! Good-bye, boy!"

He flashed his white wings and disappeared into the skeleton clouds.

"Oh, dang! Rats! *Fishcakes!*" cried Paul, disgusted. "How am I ever going to learn?"

And how was he ever going to get off this island? First, though, he needed to find the spring. Angrily kicking aside the eggshells with his bare feet, he hiked toward the hill, but no matter how far he walked, he never seemed to reach it, and soon he saw to his dismay that it was more of an inaccessible cliff than a hill.

Exhausted, his tongue feeling as big and rough as a bale of hay, Paul dropped to the ground and started to crawl on his hands and knees toward the steep brown face of the cliff. With his eyes at this level, he noticed that some of the eggshells were actually pieces of paper. And for some reason this did not surprise him at all. They might come in handy, he thought, and he stuffed several of them up his sleeve next to the survival knife. *That* might come in handy, too, if he didn't die of thirst first. Inch by painful inch he crept along.

"Water . . . , " he muttered hoarsely.

But by now the word was almost meaningless. He couldn't even call up a fantasy of water anymore.

All at once, he perceived that the cliff was not solid after all. A dark narrow crack ran from the top to the bottom of it, like a door that stands ajar, just wide enough for a slender boy to slither into. And strangely, like a door, the crack even seemed to open wider as he pushed through it. The space inside was brighter than a cave; it was more of a grotto, lighted by a shaft of sunlight from above, which gleamed on the surface of a pool.

"Ah!" cried Paul. "The spring!"

Wonderful water spurted from the rocks in a thin stream and filled Paul's mouth and throat with pure delight. Later, when he could afford the luxury of leisurely drinking, he pulled one of the sheets of paper from his pajama sleeve and folded it into a cup.

First, he made it square. Then he folded it diagonally into a triangle.

Island   53

Then he brought each of the two bottom corners across to touch the center of the opposite side.

He opened the top and folded each edge down to form the rim of the cup.

Then he put his forefinger inside and gave the bottom a little poke to flatten it.

Finally he filled it, emptied it, and drank six more cupfuls before he felt entirely himself again.

"What now?" Paul asked himself.

At least, he thought, when you were marooned on a desert island, nobody was trying to shoot you or suck out your brain. If only the albatross hadn't left him in such an utterly empty place — supplied with nothing but water, rocks, and paper! Now that his thirst was satisfied, he was beginning to feel rather hungry.

He pulled out the survival knife and examined it carefully for the first time, testing its large and small blades delicately against the ball of his thumb (they were razor sharp). But the device contained more than blades: there were also a small saw, a pair of scissors, a set of tweezers, a hammer, and a screwdriver. And that was not all. Paul also discovered a long thin tube, a sickle-shaped hook, and a curious nozzle; he couldn't imagine what their uses might be.

"But none of it is helpful at the moment," he thought, folding up the knife and marveling at how

Island

small a space all the attachments occupied. There was nothing on the island for him to hammer, saw, screw together — or eat.

"I can't eat rocks," he said aloud, wishing for a few palm trees, even though ordinarily he disliked coconut.

As soon as the words left his mouth, he felt a tremor under his feet, a deep rumble that disturbed the entire mass of mountain where he perched. He saw tiny ripples run across the surface of the spring. And although he never really heard a voice, he sensed a meaning creeping through his head, carried by the vibrations:

"Can't . . . eat . . . rocks . . . rocks . . . rocks."

It was almost like an echo, but it came from the earth, not the air. Then he felt it again, and this time the message was new. It was a question.

"Who . . . climbs . . . our . . . toes?"

"Paul," he said. His voice sounded very small. "Me, a boy. Who are you?"

Rumble, rumble, came the answer. It grew and spread until Paul tingled all over, and he began to fear that he would be caught in an earthquake.

"We . . . are . . . ROCKS . . . rocks . . . rocks."

"I never knew you could talk!" he gasped.

"ROCK-talk . . . Rock-talk . . . rrrrrrrr."

Very, very gradually the story came out. The rocks were full of meaning and rich in history, they explained, but their adventures mostly happened so slowly that other beings never noticed.

"Yet . . . we . . . see . . . everything . . ."

Paul plunked himself down flat on his stomach and laid his ear to the ground while the rock talk rumbled through every molecule in his body. Fascinated, he absorbed the story of the universe from the first crash of creation up to now — or was it the story of one grain of sand? "Hush — hush — hush," said the waves on the beach below, as they ground a grain of sand from a rock, washed it, buried it, and waited for it to become a rock again. Paul lay there listening for what might have been an hour, or what might have been a geologic age.

"Come . . ." said the rocks at last.

And Paul considered the offer. He was tempted. They were big and calm and infinitely strong, and he was small and soft and hungry. He almost wanted to be a rock. He might begin, he thought, by becoming a fossil . . . But then he heard something, an ordinary sound rather than rock talk, and he jumped up. From the crack in the cliff he could see all the way to the ocean, and there on the horizon he just made out a tiny, ship-shaped blip. The sound came again: it was the blare of a ship's horn.

"Yay! I'm saved!" shouted Paul, waving his arms.

A puff of dense black smoke rose from the funnel of the ship as the vessel sailed closer to the island, and Paul stopped waving and stared. He had seen that ship before.

Island

"Oh, no," he said. "What shall I do?"
The rocks answered.
"Be bold . . . bold . . . bold . . ."
"BEWARE . . . ware . . . ware . . . ware . . ."

Boat

"Drainers!" Paul thought
in horror.

He could not be sure, of
course; perhaps even a ship that fired on albatrosses
might be friendly to boys. Yet the gray freighter gave
him an uncanny feeling, and the rocks had told him
to beware. Since he was only one against so many,
he must depend upon his brain, which immediately
told him that there was no place on the island to
hide except inside the grotto, where thirsty sailors
— or Drainers — would be sure to find him. Then he
remembered the pieces of paper stuffed up his
sleeve. Maybe he could fly away!

Quickly, in spite of his trembling fingers, Paul
folded another Albatross. But somehow, no matter
how he tried, he couldn't quite duplicate the first
one, and when he launched the new plane, it stub-
bornly tumbled straight to the ground and lay
there. Nothing special happened at all. He tried
again and again without success.

"It's almost like it *refuses* to fly," Paul thought,
frustrated.

Maybe he had imagined the whole albatross adventure. But how else could he have gotten here? And he could still almost feel and smell the bird that had brought him to the island.

Paul peered anxiously out to sea, where the gray ship seemed to have anchored and was now launching a small boatload of men toward the shore of the island.

"A boat!" thought Paul. "Yes! I know a way to make one of those too."

He pulled out a square of paper and folded it in half.

Then he folded each half horizontally until they touched along the center line.

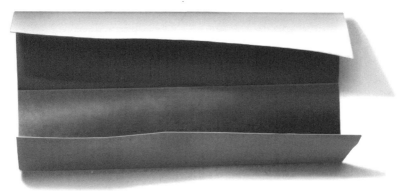

He folded each corner into a triangle, still meeting along the center line. Now the paper formed a long hexagon.

Next, Paul brought the top two corners down and the bottom two corners up to lie along the center line, creating a skinny diamond.

Boat

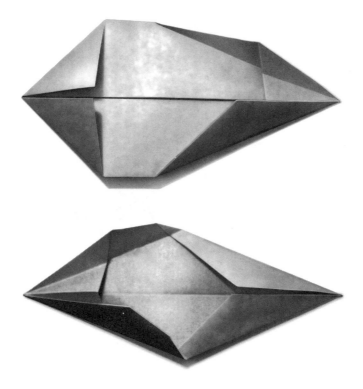

He folded the top corner of the diamond down to touch the center line, and then the bottom corner up to do the same.

Then he spread the folds and opened up the boat.

And now, slowly, delicately, he turned it inside out!

Paul's new creation rested lightly in his hand, just filling it. By now the sailors had rowed their boat quite close to shore, so that Paul could hear their voices across the waves. Although he couldn't understand what they said, or even tell what language they spoke, he was certain that he caught the word "KRON." They must be Drainers.

"I'll launch my boat from the other side of the island," he said to himself, "and try to escape before they land."

Boat

Trusting his camouflage pajamas to conceal him as he crept across the rocks, and trying not to crush the paper boat in his hand, Paul managed to climb down the cliff. It was much harder to go down than to come up.

"Just *don't think*," he ordered himself. "Especially not about the time you fell off the slide at school and broke both your arms. Or," he added sternly, "about the time you — whoops! — fell backwards — careful now, careful — into that big cactus — ouch!"

Suddenly he found himself stuck on a ledge; the reach to the next toehold was too long for his leg. His position seemed hopeless. He observed that the men in the boat wore transparent tanks on their backs and carried some kind of gear on their belts, as well as guns in their hands.

Then Paul remembered the sickle-shaped attachment on the survival knife. Perhaps if he used it as a grappling hook, anchored it in the rock, and dangled himself over the edge of the ledge, he could — yes, he *could* — reach the next foothold, and the next, and the next. Soon he stood safely at the base of the cliff, but by then the sailors had landed.

Racing from boulder to boulder, Paul immediately made his way toward the opposite side of the island, and as he ran he noticed that the paper boat seemed larger and heavier with every step. He was forced to switch it from hand to hand, and then to take short rests. Meanwhile, to his terror, he heard shouts and gunfire behind him. Had they seen him?

Or were they merely taking potshots at harmless seabirds? He stumbled onward, his arms aching from the weight of the boat.

By the time he reached the pebble beach on the far side of the albatross's island, Paul had never felt so tired in his life. He dropped the boat at the edge of the water and stared: it had become a kind of canoe or kayak, made of a hard smooth substance that he did not recognize, and it was fully large and sturdy enough to carry him. The ocean rushed forward to lick his ankles; the boat rose up and floated on the little waves.

"But," wondered Paul, "did I get smaller, or did the boat get bigger?"

There was no time to solve the riddle. He glanced fearfully over his shoulder, just in time to see a gray head pop above the hill that led to the beach, and then another, and another. He didn't wait a moment longer. Hastily he shoved the boat out to sea, leaped into it, flopped onto his stomach, and paddled with his hands as hard as he could, as though the boat were a surfboard, until he had passed the breakers. Two or three bullets zinged into the water around him. Fortunately he lay so low in the water that he made a poor target, but he knew that he was still in danger. The shots had struck awfully close. He remembered that Joe had told him that the Drainers used intelligent ammunition; "brainbullets," Joe had called them. The only way to escape was to get out of range.

Boat

"Oars!" he said to himself, panting. "Or else a paddle! How could I forget? What'll I do?"

A gust of wind gave him the answer. Paul raised his head slightly and realized that great gray whale-belly clouds were hurrying across the sky, and they were moving in the same direction that he wanted to go. He reached up his pajama sleeve and extracted another sheet of paper. It was crumpled, but he smoothed it out.

"I'll make a sail," he said.

And so he did, with a few quick folds.

But how would he hold it in place? What about ropes? Usually in situations when he needed to tie one thing to another, Paul unraveled the tops of his socks and used the thread, but today he was bare-foot. Then he remembered the scissors on his survival knife, and with two or three snips and several quick twists, he manufactured ropes and a mast from the extra paper; and then he raised the sail, which caught the wind and carried him far out to sea and safely away from the Drainers.

Manta

"The name I give to you is
Lifeboat," Paul whispered
solemnly to his craft, when
at last he felt that they had sailed beyond the range
of the gunmen.

A question occurred to him for the first time.
Why would the Drainers try to shoot their victims,
if it was live brains they wanted?

"Maybe," he thought, "they paralyze first, and
kill later, like spiders."

But Joe had bled real blood: maybe they liked to
make people hurt, too, just for the fun of it. Paul
shuddered, feeling full of uneasy, icy jangles.

The wind was blowing harder now. The clouds
had gathered close together in a mass that entirely
covered the blue sky and trailed foggy tentacles
down toward the sea, which grew choppier by the
minute. Then there was a sudden splash, and Paul
felt water in the bottom of the Lifeboat. A wave had
curled itself over the gunwales. He bailed with his
paper cup, but more waves undid his work as soon

as he finished it. His pajamas were soaked. Then, as the storm got wilder and wilder, he noticed that the boat itself was leaking and oozing and becoming soft to the touch. So it *was* paper, after all!

"Lifeboat might be the wrong name," thought Paul grimly. "'Be bold, beware,' the rocks said. Right now I could *use* a dry, solid rock or two!"

He had only one sheet of paper left, and he didn't know what to make with it. Perhaps a raft? Or else a life preserver? But would they get soggy too?

"I need something that's at home in the water," Paul decided, beginning to fold as quickly as he could. "Something that can swim . . . and something with lots of room on its back to carry me."

Here came a wave bigger than all the ones before — a wave like a huge green hill, an enormous swell topped with a whitecap like a pointed fin.

"And I need it quick!" cried Paul.

He crimped down the last fold and held the object at arm's length. What had happened? He must have missed a crucial fold, and now he was out of paper . . . and out of luck. He'd intended to make a whale. What was this huge flat creature that looked almost like an airplane instead?

At that moment the giant wave caught the lifeboat and swamped it, tossing Paul overboard and sending him wallowing into a whole new world.

At first he held his breath and sank.

But then he opened his eyes and saw silver bubbles and a strand of golden brown seaweed, and he

understood that below the surface of the ocean the
water was calm, its temperature was comfortable,
and by some miracle he was able to breathe. Or was
it that he no longer needed to breathe at all? Seawater seemed to taste like fresh air now. Stretched
on a wide, flexible surface like a trampoline, he
glided smoothly and luxuriously, as though he were
riding a hovercraft down a river rimmed with

Manta

floating flowers, in some silent, peaceful universe, far from roaring wind or crowds or engines. Then out of this deep silence he began to hear marvelous singing:

Hoooo
Eeeee
Yup-yup-yup . . .

What on earth — or under water — could it be? The weird sounds paused, and then continued.

Chirp
Chirp
ZZZZZZZ
Hoooo

Suddenly Paul's raft soared toward the surface of the ocean, gathering speed as it rose, until finally it leaped through the glassy surface and into the air. The flight was brief. Paul had just enough time to grab a quick breath before they landed with a resounding splash, and the raft gathered itself into the shape of a scoop and plunged twenty times as deep as before. It must be alive, he realized, but what kind of creature was it? He could no longer hear the far-off, fabulous music.

"Stop!" yelled Paul in a very bubbly voice, grabbing for the rippling edges of his live raft, but it slithered out of his grasp.

The creature bucked like a flat rubber bronco, and he felt himself slipping backward until he was

Manta

only hanging onto its very thin tail. Then to his great relief it reached the ocean bottom and plunked itself, and Paul, down in a cloud of sand.

"Maybe I should introduce myself," he thought, when the water had cleared somewhat.

"Excuse me," he gurgled.

"What! I thought I got rid of you! Leave me alone, you nasty little stowaway!" Quick as a wink, the creature rolled its front fins into devilish horns and glowered at him.

"I didn't mean to land on you," said Paul. "My boat sank, you see."

"That's no excuse!"

"I'm sorry," said Paul. "I know I don't belong here — "

"You're right about that! Trespasser! Troublemaker! Invader!"

"My name is Paul, and I'm a boy. Who are you?"

The creature rippled furiously all over and spat out a mouthful of sand. "I am a manta ray, of course — a *female* manta ray. Any idiot should know that."

"Wow!" said Paul. "Really? Manta rays are cool!"

The ray rippled again, less angrily, almost as though she were preening herself. "Humph!"

"I guess I was too close to see you," Paul went on, paddling a few strokes away and noticing as he swam that his hands and feet seemed thinner and more flexible than usual in the water — almost fins, in fact. He fingered his neck, searching for gills, but although the skin felt somewhat rough, he found no major change there.

Now he could make sense out of the shape lying half buried on the bottom of the sea, with its two suspicious little eyes bulging through the sand.

"Thanks for the ride," Paul said. Even with his incredible newfound ability to swim underwater without air, he felt very clumsy compared to the manta ray. "How do you move like that?" he asked.

The ray shrugged.

"Muscles, probably," mused Paul. "And with that design, you should have very little drag."

She basically flew through the water, he thought — and through the air, too.

"I," said the ray proudly, "am a *cartilaginous* fish."

"Like a giant flying doormat."

"I beg your pardon!"

"Never mind," said Paul quickly. "I'm hungry, and I'd like to go home. Can you help me?"

"Certainly not. Why should I?"

Paul finally lost his patience. "Oh, *fishcakes!*" he told the irritable manta ray. "Oops! Excuse me! I didn't mean you. Really. But I guess I don't need any help after all, thank you very much." And off he paddled.

He floated slowly across the sand, past rocks encrusted with mollusks and through writhing brown curtains of algae, until after a while he came to a reef. Deep in a crevice he glimpsed a tiny flicker

Manta

of movement, followed by a dazzling bolt of blue-white brightness.

"An electric eel!" marveled Paul, keeping his distance.

The eel turned off its light, and Paul paddled on, forgetting all his problems in his pleasure at what he saw around him. Sea anemones sprouted from the reef like frosted glass flowers and then shut up into strawberry shapes; sapphire fishes jabbed gently at the water; a violet-spotted lobster scuttled into a shadow and then turned and snapped its bristly claws at him. There were many kinds of coral too, glowing with fluorescent colors: crisp white staghorns, red roses, cocoa brown mushrooms, pale heads of cauliflower, squishy green cushions, and convoluted gray brains.

Just as Paul paused to tread water and admire the coral gardens, he sensed turbulence in the ocean behind him and whirled around, his chest tight with fear. It was the manta ray, looming over him and blocking the light like a huge wet bat.

"I have been watching you," she announced in an ominous tone.

"I haven't done anything wrong," said Paul stoutly.

To his surprise the manta ray nodded her front end. "You haven't killed anything, stolen anything, poisoned anything, or dumped any filthy rotten garbage. You haven't even touched anything."

"No."

Her tone grew sharper. "I don't *think* you work for the . . . Sea Enemy. Do you? Hmm?"

"Sea Enemy?" asked Paul. "What's that?"

She didn't answer, but her voice turned sweet. Maybe too sweet, Paul said to himself. "I think I *would* like to help you, dear boy," she said.

"Thanks," answered Paul politely.

Yet still he had his doubts. He had never heard that manta rays were famous for their tender hearts and dainty habits; he *had* heard that they used their curly horns to shovel little fishes into their mouths as fast as possible. So he stayed carefully away from her head. Nevertheless, the ray had powerboated them through the water much faster than Paul could do the flutter kick. He might also benefit from her protection and her knowledge of the world of the sea, and with luck he might just find his way home.

At that moment he heard the strange singing again.

Hoooo

Eeeee

Ohhnnnohhhnnnohh

Chirp

Manta

Song

"What *is* that?" cried Paul.

"You silly! Haven't you ever heard the song of the humpback whale?" replied the manta ray, tapping him playfully on the arm.

"No." Paul moved slightly aside and listened intently. The music seemed to be chanted through a huge distant megaphone, and although the sounds were exquisite, he had no idea what they meant.

Ohhnnnohhhnnnnohh
Ahhnnnohhhnnnnohh

"He just goes on and on," complained the manta ray. "Every year a new song, but the same song all year long. *Bor*ing, if you ask me. And he's supposed to be so smart! One of the biggest brains in the ocean, or some such nonsense! But I want to talk about *you.*" She tapped him again, somewhat harder. "Dear boy! What are we going to do? How shall I get rid — I mean, where shall I take you?"

Paul thought about it.

"Topside?" asked the manta ray eagerly.

He shook his head. Without his boat, and without any sense of his location, he would be even more lost than he was already. Alone on the surface, he would drown. And since the albatross's island had certainly been taken over by Drainers, he must stay away from there.

"I need to find North America," he said at last.

She fluttered with annoyance. "That dumb old dry geography means nothing to me, you stup — I mean, you sweet young thing. I don't go near the coasts. Much too dangerous!"

This reminded Paul of something that had puzzled him. "What did you mean by the Sea Enemy?" he asked.

"Shut up!" she snapped, rolling up her horns in a fearsome manner.

"I think I know," he said. And he whispered the name "KRON" as quietly as possible, but the manta ray still threw a terrible fit. Ten full minutes passed before all the sand settled and Paul judged that it was safe to swim out of the crevice in the rocks where he had taken refuge, along with some startled crabs. The manta ray was nowhere to be seen, but Paul guessed she hadn't gone very far away.

"Listen, Manta," he called. "Stop your fussing. We've got to work together."

She poked one eye out of the sand at his feet. "Not on your life, boy!" she snapped. "Every manta for herself!"

At last he persuaded her to listen to his idea. "Take me to the humpback whale. Whales travel all around the world, so he'll know where the continents are."

Suddenly she agreed. "Oh, all right! Just to make you happy, dear boy!"

He felt a little suspicious of such a quick change of heart, but he had already learned that the manta ray was nothing if not changeable, so he scrambled once more onto her slippery back. And with a whoosh that nearly swept him off backwards, they went on their way.

The whale's song grew gradually louder and clearer as they traveled, and Paul's understanding of it grew clearer, too. But it was not an understanding that he could put into ordinary words. The words that came into his head were odd, disconnected phrases.

thumb squeaking a balloon squeaking a balloon
moaning and groaning moaning and groaning
long long ago
long long ago
long long long long
ago

"Are you still hungry, sweet boy?" asked the manta ray after they had swum for quite a long time.

The ocean bottom was as flat here as a prairie and seemed just as endless to Paul as the Great Plains on land, which he had once seen for several long days from the back seat of a car. He didn't quite like the ray's tone of voice and would have preferred to listen to the whale music uninterrupted.

"Not very," he said.

"Wouldn't you like to have a nice little . . . squid?"

"No, thanks."

"How about a lovely . . . lobster?"

"No, thanks."

"Hmm. Oysters? Clams? No? Oh, *I* know," she whispered enticingly, *"Crab legs!"*

Paul's mother was an adventurous cook and he was a fearless eater, so he had tasted all of these things, but somehow he didn't want to tell the manta so.

"Well, then," she said, "what *do* boys like to eat?" She skidded to a halt and curled around to face him ferociously. "Is it . . . MANTA RAY?"

"No!" He burst out laughing, which offended her so much that she dumped him, and then kicked sand all over him in a fury.

"Sorry, Manta," he said, coming up coughing and spluttering. "I would never eat you. No way! In fact, my most favorite food of all is whipped cream."

He thought longingly of wonderful white puffy billows of cream. How lusciously it deflated in his mouth! How marvelously well it mixed with sweet-and-sour strawberries, and above all with squashy spicy pumpkin pie! Really, whipped cream improved anything it touched, Paul thought. He even liked to eat it all by itself.

"Sickening!" said the manta ray when he explained whipped cream to her. "Absolutely revolting!"

But she seemed more cheerful now, and Paul realized that she had been at least as afraid of him as he had been of her. He gave her a friendly pat. She flattened herself out so that he could climb back on, and away they zipped, flying through the ocean even faster than before. Soon the prairie gave way to oceanic hills and mountains, and they circled around an underwater volcano that rumbled and glowed as it poured out liquid rock that hardened instantly into crusty black tongues when it hit the seawater.

They had been cruising for a while above the deepest canyon in the world when the manta ray suggested that they take a peek inside. Paul willingly agreed.

So they dived down inside it, very deep, with Paul marveling all the time at his newfound ability to live underwater without needing air. As they dived they lost the last of the daylight, and the ocean grew pitch black. They were surrounded by all sorts of fishy beings that made their own weird light; Paul thought they looked like clumps of glow-in-the-dark cobwebs as they drifted past. It was like swimming through a haunted house. He wasn't

Song

sorry to rise up again and leave that spooky scene behind.

The whale song was much closer and clearer now:

A door in a shipwreck creaking squeaking creaking
Long long ago
Hoooo
Eeeee
O long ago O long ago
O!

The manta ray slowed down and hovered over the fragile bones of a sunken ship, half-overgrown with sea life. A white dinner plate painted with blue dragons lay on the ocean floor, but nothing else from the wreck was recognizable except for the rusty ruins of a cannon. The manta and Paul each gave a shiver and sped onward. Gradually the water grew shallower, and the whale sang louder and louder.

Bup-bup-yup-yup
Moan and groan and tone and bone and all alone
Bup-bup-bup

"Look! There he is!" said the manta ray.

The great beast hung almost vertically in the water, singing and blowing bubbles by the thousands from his blowhole. He moved slowly in a circle as he did so, and gradually the bubbles clung together and formed a huge airy tube.

"What's he doing?" asked Paul, leaning over what would have been the manta's shoulder, if she'd had one.

"Shh!" she hissed. "He's making a bubble net to catch krill."

And sure enough, Paul saw that the chains of air encircled a school of tiny animals.

"What's krill?"

"*Teeny* tiny shrimpies, silly boy. We won't bother him till he's done."

With a sudden plunge and an immense slurp, the whale inhaled his dinner, sucking the krill with gusto into his baleen strainers and then bursting into the loudest song so far.

O deep in love deep deep in love
O foghorns deep full fathom five O love
O sad O cloud of love
O burp

Then he saw them, and the music stopped.
"Who are you?" boomed the humpback whale.

Song

Humpback

Swish! As unceremoniously
as usual, the manta ray
flipped Paul off her back
and left him treading water in front of one of the
whale's enormous eyes. The animal himself was like
a living mountain, Paul thought, with his great
pleated throat and his bulky body. Inside the throat,
the baleen hung down like strange mustaches, and
the rough, spotted flippers were much longer than
Paul himself.

"In spite of your puny size, you appear to be an
immature example of some species of marine mammal," remarked the whale in deep tones not unlike
his singing voice. "You are neither an invertebrate
nor a fish. You have hair, like me."

"Yes, sir," gurgled Paul. And then he thought nervously to himself, "Dang! He's as long as a double
tractor-trailer rig!"

"There are thirty-seven hairs in my beard," said
the whale complacently, although his many square
feet of snout appeared to be entirely smooth.

"My father has a beard," Paul volunteered. "But I don't, not yet. I'm still a child, you see, sir."

The whale said nothing, but smiled hugely. At least he was not the kind of whale with sharp teeth, thought Paul. Then he told himself, "Be bold," and he spilled out his story to the humpback. Meanwhile the manta ray lurked at a distance.

"We must take action," rumbled the whale when Paul was done.

"If I could get back to my bedroom and find KRON, I think I know what I would do next. But how — "

The whale raised a flipper. "One moment, please. This requires careful consideration."

He rolled over and floated in silence for several minutes while Paul waited as calmly as he could. He was beginning to feel uneasy and wondered how the war was going without him. And . . . was that a shark, flashing palely just at the edge of his vision? Bit by bit, the manta ray came slipping back through the water and waited with him until the whale delivered his opinion.

"I agree that we cannot simply carry you Topside and leave you, child. You are a lesser mammal, not a whale. I fear that you would indeed drown. Instead I propose to convey you as close as possible to your home, and I have confidence that you will find your own way from there."

"But do you think I'll be able to breathe air again?" asked Paul anxiously. "And will I get the bends when I come up?"

The whale blew a few thoughtful bubbles. "Of course, I cannot say for sure, but I believe that whatever power it was that enabled you to survive beneath the sea will not fail you on the land."

Besides, Paul thought, what choice did he have, really?

"Let's go, sir," he said. "Good-bye, Manta, and thank you."

Waving her entire rubbery self, she called back, "Good-bye, dear boy! Good luck!"

And this time Paul felt sure she meant it.

Paul immediately found that the difference between a whale and a manta ray is as big as the difference between an elephant and a lily pad. All the small fry of the sea cleared out of their way as they traveled, with Paul positioned in a hollow of the whale's back. The whale sang as he swam, and Paul thought he would never tire of lying there with his ear to the massive animal's back, lulled by his music.

O sad and sweet
Never ever never ever never
O why O die
O ZZZZZZZ
Na na na na.

What was that? Paul jerked himself up to a sitting position. Had he fallen asleep, and had his Voice crept into a nightmare? He stared all around but saw nothing to frighten him. The humpback whale sang again.

Humpback

Eeeee
Hoooo
Na na na na na.

"Sir!" cried Paul, drumming on the whale's skin
with his hands and feet. "Danger! Danger!"

"Eh?"

"KRON, sir. It's somewhere near. I can hear it."

"Where?"

That was the question. Was it too late? Was
KRON already inside the whale? Or was KRON plan-
ning to capture this powerful creature by infiltrating
first his song, and then the rest of his enormous
brain?

"What a trophy a whale brain would be!"
thought Paul, horrified.

It must not be allowed to happen. There was too
much at stake, including Paul's own head. Yet how
difficult it was to fight an invisible enemy! Just as he
nearly despaired, he caught a glimpse of green-and-
blue clay and bits of plastic. Like a little submarine,
almost close enough for Paul to touch, KRON sank
past the whale.

Paul saw that one of KRON's weapons was really
a micropump, and he realized in a flash that the
clay monster must be searching for the whale's ear.
Paul's own brain worked at top speed.

"A whale's ear is very hard to find," he reasoned
to himself, "and KRON seems to be alone."

Moving as quietly as possible, he drew out his

survival knife, pushed away from the whale, and followed the clay figure. So far, KRON had failed to find any trace of an ear, but now it seemed to be heading for the whale's blowhole. At the sight of this, Paul did not hesitate, and with one swift pounce he slashed off KRON's micropump. It tumbled harmlessly through the water.

Instantly KRON began to spew a gray-brown substance from the muzzles of his other guns, which hid him from Paul and clouded the water around the humpback whale. Then the cloud hardened into a pattern, taking a larger shape almost as the bubbles had done when the whale used them to catch the krill. But this object was a solid net, a fisherman's net, and it grew larger and tighter and more tangled and impenetrable before Paul's eyes. It was a real hazard even to a whale.

"Swim!" Paul cried.

"How?" moaned the whale, who was now imprisoned from head to tail.

But the knife was still in Paul's hand. With the little saw blade, he attacked the net wildly, although without much hope, and then to his amazement the loops melted beneath the serrated edge as if it were red-hot.

"It must be a laser!" thought Paul.

Avoiding the whale's quivering skin, he sawed again and again until he had cut a pathway through the net to the open water, and the whale gave a tremendous flip of his flukes and shot through the hole, grunting mightily. Just then Paul saw a whole fleet of Drainers spurt from KRON's clay stomach and head toward him: little gray soldiers swimming quickly underwater without any visible signs of scuba gear, although each one was armed with a micropump.

"Wait!" he called to the whale, who seemed not to hear. Bubbles rose from his blowhole. What was he doing? Perhaps he was in shock, thought Paul, or perhaps KRON had gotten to the creature after all.

Paul knew he was on his own.

The knife was still in his hand, but he was badly outnumbered, and the Braindrainers were gaining on him. Then he felt a sharp stab in his chest. He looked down and saw that one of the Drainers had hit him with a smartspear. Luckily this one was tiny, little more than a dart, so he plucked it out and continued to swim as fast as he could toward the whale.

But now there was blood in the water.

Another smartspear grazed Paul's ribs. Feeling extremely tired, he knew that soon he would have to make a stand against the Drainers. But as his body weakened, his courage grew stronger and stronger.

"At least I'll take a few of 'em down with me!" he vowed. Turning, he raised his survival knife.

One, two! One, two! With long strokes of the big blade he demolished the first few Drainers, micropumps and all. Bits and pieces of them drifted away in the water. But new ones kept on coming like mosquitoes, and no matter how he batted at them, he could not keep them away from his face. And KRON was with them now. All at once Paul felt a needle puncture his ear, and he heard the terrible Voice at full volume.

Na na na na. Na na na na.

For one single instant, Paul was filled with awful pain, as though every nerve in his body was being pulled out by the roots. Then, with his last scrap of strength, he seized the dreaded clay figure, which deformed at the touch of his hands, and he flung it as far away from himself as he could.

And then a tremendous shove lifted Paul up and rammed him through the water, away from KRON, and the Drainers, and the fever Voice — upward and upward for what seemed like forever — until he broke through the surface with a gasp. Within easy swimming distance, waves were lapping onto a tropical beach, and in the blue sky above his head fat white clouds were arranged like cushions.

"Air!" he said and took a gulp of it. After water, it seemed perhaps a little . . . thin. But he was sure that he could get used to it again.

The whale, who had butted him all the way up, now breached beside him and blew a tall column of fishy-smelling spray into the air. He landed in the water again with a giant splash.

"What happened?" yelled Paul, rocked by the ripples.

"I surrounded them with a bubble net, child,"

Humpback

replied the whale. He drew a breath big enough to inflate a hot-air balloon. "Extricating *you* from the Braindrainers without inadvertently liberating *them* required considerable agility on my part, if I say so myself."

"It was awesome, sir. But — but — what happened to the Drainers?"

The whale grinned broadly, and for once his response was brief.

"Sharks," he said.

Virus

"Paul!"

It was a voice from the past, a voice he never expected to hear again.

"Dad!"

"What are you doing?"

"Well, uh," said Paul, discovering to his great surprise that the ocean had vanished. He was standing, perfectly dry, arms outstretched, in the middle of his bedroom floor, surrounded by clumps of dirty clothes and scraps of paper. Where had all that water gone?

"I was marooned on a desert island, and then I went under the sea, and I just came up," said Paul in a rush.

Dad's eyebrows shot up so far that they almost touched his hair.

"I was pretending," Paul added, feeling a little sheepish, and the eyebrows came down again.

Dad stroked his beard and nodded thoughtfully. Without being told, Paul knew that his father was concerned about him, which made him feel rather important yet frightened about himself at the same time.

"It's lunchtime," Dad said after a moment.

Paul's own room looked almost unfamiliar: could that pile of socks be the albatross's island? And what had happened when the sharks ate the Drainers? Then he remembered that sharks could swallow almost anything with no ill effects. He himself seemed to have lost all the hunger that he'd felt earlier.

"I'm thirsty," he said, pressing his hand to his shoulder, which ached, and so did his shins, as though he had been running a long-distance race. He noticed a slight greasy film of modeling clay on his fingers.

Dad tested the temperature of his cheek. "No wonder. You're burning up."

He went into the bathroom and filled a glass at the basin. The cool tap water rushed down Paul's throat, tasting almost as good as a magical spring on a desert island.

"I think it's time for your medicine," remarked Dad, tapping a pill from the bottle.

His calm, everyday behavior had a good effect. The world where they stood grew bigger and brighter, and the other world dwindled into something colorless and incomplete, like last night's dream.

"Dad," said Paul, "why do I feel like this?"

"You're fighting some kind of infection, and a

high fever dehydrates you and plays games with your head. If you're not better soon, I'm going to call the doctor."

Then they went into the kitchen, which was full of shiny objects whose brightness pained Paul's aching eyes. He felt as though he were observing the world — this world, anyway — from a high, distant, lonesome place, like the top of a tower.

"But why do bad things happen? Why are there viruses?"

"Those are very big questions," said Dad, which Paul knew was either the beginning of a long and complicated answer or a complete, short, and sideways one. Both kinds were somewhat unsatisfactory, Paul felt, and he sighed. He supposed he would just have to find out for himself, and sure enough, without further ado, Dad opened the refrigerator and peered inside.

"Tuna salad?" he suggested.

Paul recoiled. "No!" The manta ray would never forgive him, he thought.

Dad's eyebrows went up again. "How about chicken soup?"

"Too hot."

"Hmm. Well, I think your mom made you some Jell-O."

Whipped cream was good on Jell-O — or rather, Jell-O was a good excuse to have whipped cream. Paul looked to see if by some miracle his mother had remembered this, but she had not. Even though she was a very intelligent woman, he simply could not make her understand the vital importance of whipped cream. He ate the Jell-O anyway, and just as he was scraping the dish, his mother telephoned from work.

"He's about the same," Dad told her. "Want to say hello?"

Paul put the receiver to his ear, and his mother's voice poured warm and comfortable words over the place where KRON had stuck the micropump.

"Back to bed," said his father as soon as Paul hung up. They passed Dad's study, where the untended computer sat simmering like a teakettle on a slow fire.

"Dad, what if all the computers in the world got taken over?"

"Taken over by what?"

"I don't know exactly. Something like a virus."

"Well," said Dad, "that would be dangerous. Whether they're electronic or alive, brains *are* power. And power is easy to abuse. Now, hop into bed and see if you can take a nap, and I'll bet you wake up feeling better. No more desert islands, okay?"

"But surely that didn't mean 'no more paper folding,'" thought Paul, once he was under the covers again.

He picked up a sheet of orange tissue paper, which crinkled faintly at the touch and reminded him of autumn leaves. But instead of making something out of it, he let it drift down onto the bedspread while he gazed idly out the window. Beneath the noonday sun, the mountains looked quite flat, no thicker than a backdrop on a stage.

"I might have cut them out of purple sandpaper," thought Paul dreamily, "and glued them on the sky."

Clouds appeared, many little streams and rivulets of them, joining rapidly into a pattern. As they passed across the sky from south to north, the pattern sprang into focus: it was a tree. The tree of clouds blew over the mountains and disappeared.

Skree — ee — eek.

That was the sound of a real tree, the one outside Paul's window. Dad was always saying that he was going to prune the branch that rubbed against the windowpane, but so far he hadn't. Sometimes when it scraped on the glass at night it made an almost scary sound — if you didn't know what it really was, that is.

Paul decided that the orange tissue paper was asking to be cut into a shape, but where were his scissors? "Why did scissors never stay where you left them? Probably Katie had stolen them," he thought indignantly, forgetting how many times he had raided Katie's drawers and his parents' desks. He rummaged in his craft box without success before he remembered the tiny scissors on the survival knife.

But the knife was gone. The only thing inside his pajama sleeve was his own arm. "Maybe I dropped it when the whale bumped me," he thought sadly.

Then he remembered KRON. How could he have forgotten to search for the evil clay figure? Everyone was depending on him, and here he was, stupidly lollygagging in bed! Paul crossed the room in three leaps and hunted through the clutter in the closet from top to bottom, but he found no trace at all of a blue-and-green clay figure, except for a grease spot on the edge of the shelf where KRON used to sit and dangle its legs. Then he thought back to the fight underwater. At the end of it, where had he flung his opponent?

Perhaps KRON had landed elsewhere in the room. Almost as soon as Paul began to search the floor, he found the survival knife, lying hidden under yesterday's underwear. Chills ran up and down his backbone as he touched it; in fact he grew so cold that he jumped back into bed and pulled the covers up to his chin.

When he opened the knife, it didn't seem quite as amazing as he expected. It looked almost like an ordinary Swiss Army knife. But it did include scissors, and almost without a plan he took up the tissue paper and snipped at it until he had produced a simple winged shape. Very, very delicately he creased it down the middle with his thumbnail and, with that single stroke, transformed it into a small orange airplane, feather-light. To add just a bit of weight, he taped a single match head from his secret stash to the top of the fuselage near the nose.

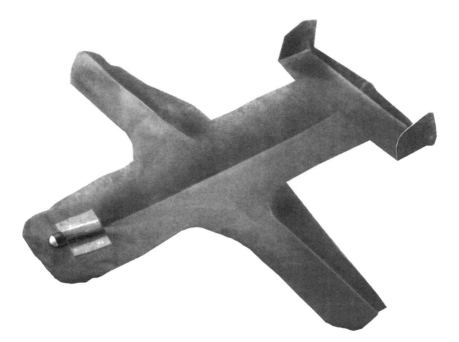

Then he balanced it upon the back of his hand and launched it with the smallest possible backward jerk. The tissue-paper plane flew slowly and delicately, wafting its way to the ground like a brilliant butterfly. And that was that.

"Now what?" thought Paul.

He felt terribly flat, and also rather sleepy. Was it all over? Was it time (oh, dang!) to start catching up on his homework?

"No!" he said aloud.

Miraculously all his sleepiness disappeared.

Virus

KRON must be hiding somewhere, maybe even in the mountains, where he would pose a grave threat to the green soldiers. Maybe it was time to make another big plane, a whole bird instead of just a feather, and one that could fly reconnaissance missions.

"What about an eagle?" he thought.

And he folded the Eagle in a special way that made it fast and strong; he could hardly wait to see how it would fly. It was a war plane, and he would use it to finish off the Braindrainer army and, if possible, their leader too.

Eagle

This time, Paul deliberately armed himself, slipping his knife up his sleeve and putting together a bulletproof vest from several sheets of heavy construction paper. He also used the cotton from the pill bottle to make himself a pair of earplugs. Then he took a deep breath and climbed aboard the Eagle. He had a feeling that some dark and difficult adventure awaited him, and it would be a long time before he came home from this flight, if indeed he ever did.

But go he must. He had made KRON. He must unmake KRON.

The cockpit was filled with incredibly complicated instruments, some of which could actually read Paul's own thoughts, and they quickly taught him how to operate them. The takeoff went like clockwork. He was astonished by the Eagle's powerful lift: before Paul blinked twice, they had soared so high that the world below was toy sized. Paul might almost have constructed it himself. The houses were tiny colored blocks, the trees were tufts of lichen, and the swimming pools were turquoise gems. Cars moved along the roads like beads on strings. The fields were quilts of brown and green and gold.

"Why do miniatures look so perfect?" wondered Paul as he flew. "I guess all the dirt and cracks of real life don't show."

He activated the Eagle Vision apparatus and gasped with amazement, for it worked like a microscope and telescope combined in one instrument. Now he could see little birds hiding in the treetops and rabbits frozen with fright under shrubs. He peered through windows and down chimneys; he watched people doing chores and having fights, playing soccer and lying in hospital beds. Ordinary. Or was it?

He fine-focused the Eagle Vision and dropped with a gasp into another dimension. He found himself flying into a human brain. This landscape — or brainscape — reminded him of the coral reef; it teemed with bizarre shapes, some beautiful and some almost unbearably awful.

"Better not look," he warned himself. "Now let's get out of here!"

As he fumbled with the controls, he somehow managed to turn on the sound. At first it was a loud yammer that filled his own head with confusion, in spite of the earplugs, but then the static died away and individual noises became clear. Wind blew, bacon sizzled, and bits of poetry recited themselves:

One, if by land, and two, if by sea;
And I on the opposite shore will be . . .

"Here," said voice after voice; "Here," "Here," "Here," as though they were answering roll call in school. And then it came, the sound that Paul hated.

Na. Na na na.

"Where are you?" he yelled. "Go away!"

He paused to listen. He had never spoken back to the Voice before. What would happen?

Nothing happened. Paul waited breathlessly, thinking that at least he had found KRON, even though he didn't know what to do next.

Na NA na na na.

This time the Voice sounded almost like mocking laughter. And Paul realized that, like the incredible flight instruments, it was tapping into his mind; it was already inside his brain. Was this the end, then?

"Am I drained?" he thought. "But how can I be? I'm still thinking, I'm still fighting. And I'm still Paul!"

And now a new sound cut through the commotion, a raucous yelping bark: "Kya! Kya!"

The evil Voice wobbled, and so did Paul, for now the airplane jabbed, plunged, and recovered like a boxer's fist.

"Kya!" came the cry again, this time almost in Paul's ear, and the cockpit ripped open. Outside air rushed over him like a cold shower.

Eagle

Paul's first thought as he fell was: "Dang! I should have made myself a parachute, not a bulletproof vest!"

Then he remembered how Dad had said that gravity was his enemy, and then he wondered where, and in what world, he would land. Just as he was thinking that a deep snowdrift would be nice, but afterwards unpleasantly cold and wet (although perhaps he could build himself an snow cave), he was jerked to a halt. A set of huge hooks seized him from behind and held him dangling in midair by the seat of his pajamas.

"Oh, no," groaned Paul, craning his neck to see what had caught him. The hooks in his pants were iron talons, which were attached to the end of heavily feathered bird legs, which in turn were attached to a very large golden eagle with the sharpest beak and steeliest eyes that Paul had ever seen. Still dangling him like a hapless rabbit, the eagle cruised toward a high rocky promontory.

"I suppose," Paul thought glumly, "they don't actually eat their prey in the air. Well, I'm a goner now. Out of the fire and into the frying pan."

But he was not destined to become eagle food. The great bird laid him down on the rocks with care and perched beside him. Then the two yellow blades of the beak opened, but instead of "Kya!" a melodious alto voice went straight to business: "KRON has crossed the Barrier. Are you ready to follow?"

Paul looked the eagle in the eye and knew that he was addressing the queen and commander in chief of the air.

"I'm afraid there will be trouble," he said.

The eagle shrugged. "There is always trouble. What matters is how you stand up to it."

She tilted her head sideways and measured him with her fierce gaze; Paul felt uncomfortably small, and he wondered what his parents would say about the holes in the seat of his pajamas.

"Was that a brainplane?" he asked.

"Not when you first made it. Somehow KRON must have broken in, but that plane won't bother us again." With the tip of one wing she pointed out a white heap on the ground far below them.

"You downed it? Gee, thanks!"

She inclined her head slightly. "We will need reinforcements. We must call up the hawks, and, I think, the condors also. They are few but formidable. And we must cross the Barrier as soon as we can, for KRON is already on its way to the mountains. Are you ready?"

Paul adjusted his earplugs and his vest, checked his survival knife, and nodded; his voice seemed frozen somewhere in his chest.

"Do not be afraid. There is safety in valor."

The eagle commander picked him up again, flapped her broad wings, and soared, gaining speed without apparent effort. The Barrier loomed up squarely in front of them, much more forbidding than Paul had imagined, and he couldn't help shutting his eyes for a moment as they pushed through it and splashed into a fresh new place on the other side. When he dared to peek again, the eagle was floating serenely above a dense forest, and the purple sandpaper mountains he had seen earlier had grown three-dimensional, brown, and almost close enough to touch. Cliffs of astonishing height and steepness overlooked the woods, and above the cliffs a sequence of ledges rose like stairs to the crest of the mountains, which seemed to crack the top of the earth's atmosphere and touch outer space.

"We've almost reached your fort," said the eagle.

And sure enough, Paul recognized the broad tree-top that served as a roof for his tree fort. The eagle dived through the branches with breathtaking skill, not bending a single stem, and landed them both safely on the platform. There Paul was glad to find the airtight ammunition box that contained his fort equipment, with everything intact inside. His army canteen sat beside it, still full.

"We'll take cover here for a little while," the eagle said, "and plan our strategy."

"Shh," came a soft voice.

"I didn't say anything," said Paul.

"Shh," came the voice again.

The eagle raised her wing in a gesture of warning.

"Shhhhhhh." The tree swayed slightly, although Paul hadn't noticed any wind, and he realized the noise was coming from the leaves. In order to hear better, he removed his earplugs.

"Is it KRON?" he said, alarmed.

The eagle laid one claw on his arm, and Paul immediately squeezed his lips together tightly.

"The leaves are whispering to us," hissed the eagle. "Listen."

Tree

The leaves talked faster than the rocks, and they all spoke at once but said different things, with occasional creaks and groans from the branches, so that Paul had a good deal of trouble following the conversation. In spite of all the hours that he had spent in trees, none of them had ever spoken to him before. Luckily the eagle understood tree language much better than Paul did; she could even pick up a few messages from the roots. Trunks, Paul gathered, remained silent (until they split — or burned.)

KRON had very recently passed through the forest, some of the leaves said. No, no, insisted others, that was hours ago, or yesterday, or perhaps last month. Other leaves added that a whole flock of thinkerchoppers had crossed overhead, and many other aircraft too, either before or after their clay commander.

"And what about Drainers?" asked Paul.

"Yes. No. Only a few. They dropped their

cigarettes and set a fire. No, they didn't. Help, help, here they come!"

But as far as Paul could tell, the forest was empty of all beings except for plants, animals, and himself.

"Leaves, you are contradicting one another, as usual," said the eagle severely. "The roots tell me that the ground shook when KRON's army passed through about an hour ago."

"That's just what we said. No, it isn't. Yes, it is."

As the trees continued their argument, stirred up by every breeze that blew, she turned her attention to Paul.

"I will do aerial reconnaissance," she said. "You stay here, make preparations, and hold the fort. We must assemble the raptors."

And with a leap and a rustle of her strong dry quills, she was gone. Paul watched the dark speck until it dissolved into the blue sky. Then he opened his ammunition box, took out his supplies, and turned to his work, making additional eagles, speedy falcons, husky hawks, and wide-winged, high-flying condors just as rapidly as his hands could fold them. He lined them up in rows on the tree house floor, ready for the great battle to come. Then he inspected his catapult, which seemed to be in good working order, and prepared a pile of ammunition.

"I don't think Dad meant I couldn't make *this* kind of bomb," he thought. "Besides, it's an emergency situation."

Just as he laid the last bomb on the pile, someone

hammered on his trap door: "Rat-tat-tat-tat!"

He peered over the railing but saw nobody and heard nothing unusual. The rope ladder dangled freely; the trees talked quietly among themselves.

"Rat-tat-tat-tat!"

Now he saw it. It was a black-and-white woodpecker with a red head, not nearly as big a bird as the queen of eagles but larger than Paul, and with a beak as long as a jackhammer.

"You!" the woodpecker shrieked, plainly in a rage. "You're the one who nailed a woodpecker wing to his bedroom wall!"

"But I never killed it," said Paul, backing away from the furious bird. "It was the cat."

The woodpecker drummed again, this time close to Paul's feet.

"And whose cat was it?"

"Well — mine, I guess, although cats mainly belong to themselves. But I never wanted Scout to kill birds. I was really sorry about the woodpecker, but by the time I found it, there was nothing I could do."

"It! It was no it! It was my uncle!"

"I *am* sorry," said Paul.

"Rat-tat-tat-tat. I should squash you like the bug you are!"

"Please don't. I have to stop KRON."

The woodpecker stopped hammering and glared at Paul suspiciously; he looked ready to skewer the boy at any moment with his furious beak.

"KRON, KRON. Everybody's talking about

KRON, but it doesn't matter to *me* one way or the other. I'm staying out of it. I bet KRON's only a figment of your imagination, anyhow."

There was a sudden crackle among the dry leaves and twigs on the ground near the foot of the tree, and both Paul and the woodpecker stiffened. Together they watched a panther come stalking through the shrubs and saplings, a black shape just a little darker and denser than a shadow. They saw him stop, raise his head, and sniff the breeze coming from their direction.

"Whoops," said the woodpecker. "See you later, bub!" He whisked open his checkered wings, flew to a high branch, and called down a taunt: "If there *is* any 'later' for you!"

Then with one last harsh cry, he flew away and left Paul alone with the panther.

Paul thought, "I'm not much bigger than a mouse now. Will he remember me? Should I call to him? Should I keep quiet?"

But it was too late. The panther lifted his huge mint-green eyes and stared straight at Paul.

"Nice kitty," said Paul. "Nice Scout."

"Prr-ow," murmured the panther softly, deep in his throat. He lashed his tail from side to side, and Paul knew what that meant: a pounce, soon. He also knew what Scout hated most in the whole world.

"Sorry, kitty," he said. "I wish I didn't have to do it."

And he pulled back the elastic cord of his catapult with all his strength, and fired.

"Bombs away!"

The red water balloon soared in a high arc over the treetops until it finally burst into fine explosion of water droplets, which completely soaked the panther. He jumped sideways and shook like a dog.

"SSSSsssss!"

"Fire again!" shouted Paul.

The green water balloon was a dud. But the blue one convinced the soggy panther to beat a hasty retreat.

"Whew!" sighed Paul. "Well, no harm done. He'll soon dry off. But man, oh, man, I sure do wish that eagle would come back."

He did not have long to wait before the next visitor arrived, but it was not the eagle. This time the trees gave the alarm: "Something's coming. No, all clear. Hush, hush. Watch and wait. All quiet. Yes, no, something's here!"

The white wolf appeared out of nowhere, crossed the clearing on silent paws, sat down near the foot of Paul's tree, and looked up. It was the strangest animal he had ever seen. Instead of being made of smooth curves, its body was composed of angles, and its coat was more crumpled than furry. Its legs and tail were stiff, and they crinkled as it moved; its ears pricked up in sharp triangles. Eeriest of all, it had no eyes and nose. It was entirely white.

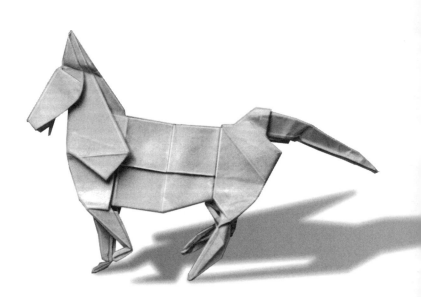

"Why, it looks like . . . but it *couldn't* be . . . "
thought Paul.

But it was a paper wolf. When it opened its
mouth and snarled, its teeth were paper too, but
sharp.

"Dang! You'd die of paper cuts!" thought Paul.

The snarl sounded horribly real. And the wolf
was huge — as large as a Shetland pony, Paul
guessed. At least wolves couldn't climb trees, he told
himself stoutly. Perhaps paper ones were different,
though; perhaps they could even fly? He squinted
down at this beast and decided not, since he saw no
sign of wings, and there was surely too much weight
and drag in that thick body for it to achieve liftoff.

Nevertheless, Paul was treed. The wolf crept

nearer and nearer, constantly making a low rumbling, crackling sound. It was too close to be attacked with the catapult, and anyhow Paul suspected that a wolf, unlike a panther, wouldn't mind getting wet.

Then he remembered his snare. Partly just for fun, and partly as a prank to catch Katie if she ever tried to invade his tree fort, he had constructed a network of twine, pulleys, and weights at the foot of the ladder. When the trap was tripped, a bent branch would snap up, balanced rocks would fall down and, if all went well, the invader would be caught securely in a lasso of string. This would do no damage to a feisty eight-year-old girl, or to a flesh-and-blood wolf, but a paper wolf might be different. The only problem was how to lure the animal into the trap.

He tried whistling: "Whee-WHEW!"

This attracted the wolf, all right; he gave a running leap and pawed sharply at the tree trunk, his muzzle snapping only inches from Paul's toes.

"Oh, *fishcakes!*" muttered Paul.

For now the wolf was on the opposite side of the tree from the snare.

"I need bait," thought Paul. "What can I use?"

Nothing heavy, he reasoned; that would set off the trap. What did paper wolves eat? He tried dropping scraps of paper one by one over the snare, but the beast paid no attention. Then in desperation

Paul crawled halfway down the ladder and dangled his own bare foot within easy reach of the paper fangs.

Whoosh! Thunk!

He closed his eyes and scrambled wildly away from the wolf. When he reached the top of the ladder he turned and found to his joy that the paper wolf was swinging from the branch, as tangled in string and helpless as a grounded kite. It continued to roar and snap, however, until he doused it with the remaining water in his canteen. Slowly it subsided into a lump of papier-mâché.

Condor

The eagle plummeted out
of the sky with no warn-
ing at all.

"Whew!" Paul thought. "Good thing I'm not a
rabbit."

He picked himself up from the floor where she
had toppled him, feeling rather dusty and stunned.

"We have no time to spare," barked the queen of
eagles. "KRON and the Braindrainer army are
attacking our forces in the mountains. Now's the
day, and now's the hour! Bring on the raptors!"

Paul pointed to the white rows of them lined up
on the treehouse floor.

"Kya!" cried the eagle, and she spread her wings
and leaped back into the air. As her shadow passed
over the paper planes, they started to rise also, and
to grow larger, and to sprout heads and legs and
feathers and brilliant golden eyes. Dozens of wings
beat in unison; shadow after shadow passed over
Paul's head and melted into the sky.

"Take me with you!" Paul begged, but the only

one that paused was a condor with a kink in its wing and which was having trouble taking off.

"Let me help," said Paul, running up and straightening the condor's wing. "Won't you let me come?" he pleaded when he was done. "You're so big you'll never notice my weight. And I must come! I must!"

The condor cranked its flat, bald, orange head around to face Paul, stared at him, and then croaked in a melancholy voice that reminded him of his Great Aunt Ethel, "Oh, very well, get on. What can I say? This kind of thing always happens to me. The others always get off scot-free, and I'm the one with extra burdens, as usual. But this isn't a picnic, young man. Don't say I didn't warn you."

She flapped once or twice, and this time she succeeded in taking off, with Paul clinging to her back. She was enormous, and she held her wings so straight that the flight was extremely smooth and very much less nerve-wracking than being dangled from the eagle's talons.

"Wow, she's a jumbo jet," thought Paul, settling down to enjoy the flight, in spite of all his worries.

They left the forest behind and soared above the mountains. At such an altitude, the rugged bare rocks below seemed merely wrinkled, and Paul began to feel lightheaded from lack of oxygen, or perhaps from listening to the condor's conversation.

"This really isn't my kind of thing at all," the condor insisted. "Not my cup of tea, no sirree.

I usually come in and clean up the mess afterward. But that eagle gets everything her own way, and when she says 'Fly,' she thinks the rest of us ought to say, 'How high?' So here I am. Yes, ma'am. No,

Condor

ma'am. No excuse, ma'am. That's what that eagle likes to hear, but it's not quite so simple in real life, is it, young man?"

"No, ma'am."

"Take this KRON thing, now. Oh, yes, I go along. I don't want to rock the boat. Not me. But it'll all be the same in a thousand years, won't it?"

"Are you sure about that?" said Paul. "Shouldn't we try to make things better?"

"We condors have problems closer to home, that's what I say. Stick to your knitting. Paddle your own canoe. I myself was just quietly perching around after a nice lunch, minding my own business, doing my level best not to go extinct, when the call came. As usual, it's a matter of life and death. The end of the world and all that. Oh, yes. So here I am, good old condor that I am, bringing up the rear, as usual, *and* doing the baby-sitting."

Paul was just going to protest that he was not a baby when he spotted some of the other raptors up ahead, and a dogfight in progress.

"Here we go," lamented the condor. "Party time. Fun and games. Drainers at four o'clock high. *Just what I expected!*"

Swiftly the Braindrainers' planes bore down upon them, bombarding the birds with rockets as they came. Paul plastered himself flat onto the condor's back and gripped her feathers as hard as he could while she wheeled sharply and dive-bombed the brainplanes. One of the planes exploded, and the condor dodged the fireball, although she singed a wing as she escaped, and Paul felt the heat crisping the fine hair on his arms. In spite of her size, the condor maneuvered surprisingly well.

Paul's stomach flipped sickeningly. Off at a distance he could hear the high-pitched screams of eagles and the harsher yells of hawks, the fierce wails of falcons, and, loudest of them all, the alto voice of the great eagle as she sang her wordless battle song. The air war was ferocious and bitter; burnt and bloody feathers tumbled toward the ground, and so did flaming bits of broken airplanes, and gray arms and legs.

Paul felt sicker and sicker; he wondered how much longer he could manage to hold onto the condor's back before he fell too. Then he noticed that she was losing altitude. They had entered into a long glide that was carrying them down and out of the fight.

"What's the matter?" he gasped. "Are you wounded?"

"No," said the condor faintly. Scraps of words floated back to Paul over the battle noise: "Exhausted . . . extra weight . . . straw that broke the camel's back . . . burden . . . just as I predicted . . . extinct."

Paul felt horribly guilty, as well as alarmed. What could he do? He glanced over his shoulder and saw to his great dismay that one of the remaining brainplanes had peeled away from the others and was coming after them. Remembering the brain-sucking micropumps, he pulled his survival knife from his sleeve and got ready for combat. Meanwhile the condor sank lower every second.

"Flap!" he cried out to her.

"Too . . . tired!"

Neither lift nor drag was the problem here, Paul realized; thrust was what they needed. How could he possibly provide it? At his back he heard the drone of the Drainer plane hurrying nearer, nearer — and without much hope he opened the survival knife and spread out the attachments. That nozzle: what was it, after all? Almost unconsciously he squeezed the handle of the knife and was astounded to find that the ruby flame decoration was in fact a concealed button, and when it was pressed, a powerful force spurted from the nozzle and propelled the condor forward with a roar.

"Jumping Jehoshaphat!" she spluttered. "Hold onto your hat, young man! Steady as she goes! There's life in the old girl yet!"

"Hooray! It's a jet engine!" shouted Paul.

Now the condor was *really* a jumbo jet. With Paul controlling the engine, and the condor piloting, they knocked the brainplane out of the sky with one blow. And then they roared to the aid of the other birds. Soon after that, the air war was over.

"Well done, raptors," called the eagle, gathering her troops about her for a meeting in midair. The rocks below them were littered with smoldering wreckage and fallen plumage. "That was the last of KRON's aircraft. Now follow me, up and away! We must provide cover for the land war. Kya! Kya!"

"'Follow me!'" grumbled the condor as they jetted along behind the eagle. "Typical! Who's the one with the latest technology, I'd like to know? Who's the one who was specially selected to carry *you*, young man! Young man! What are you doing? Stop it this minute!"

Paul had decided to try aerobatics.

"Whee!" he shouted, and away they flew.

And how they flew! They looped-the-loop, they rolled, they skimmed the mountaintop and tickled the stars, they flew sideways and upside down and backwards, they spun on their noses and twirled on their tails, until the condor pleaded for mercy and the eagle cast a disapproving backward glance.

"Take care. KRON's army is entrenched in the crags above these cliffs," she announced in ringing tones.

Flying sedately now, Paul stared at the formidable stairway to the sky, but he saw no trace of Drainers. The long afternoon was drawing to a close, and the light grew more golden as it faded from the clear blue sky. Shadows like long purple scarves appeared on the mountains.

"They have drilled their way deep into the stone," explained the eagle. "Our intelligence believes that KRON is directing operations from the center of the mountain. The Green army has cut off all apparent Drainer escape routes, but this war is not over yet. Raptors, keep your distance from the crags and be prudent while I confer with the other generals."

Paul dismounted from the condor, glad to stretch his legs.

"Well, I like that!" sniffed the condor. "After all we did, not a word of thanks. Just left in the dust! I might have guessed it would end like this. Of course, the Green army is *mostly* generals, except for us. I might as well go home and eat leftovers."

"Oh, no, you don't," said Paul as he stroked her ruffled feathers. "We're a team, remember? I won't let you leave without me."

"Humph!"

"And I think they still need us. Look!"

The council of war had ended. With the eagle waddling grandly in their midst, the Green generals were coming toward them. And to Paul's great surprise and pleasure, he saw that the youngest general, who wore one arm in a sling, was Joe.

Cliff

"Hey, kid. How's the mad
bomber?"

"Well, Barbie actually
threw it," said Paul modestly.

"She *did?* Unbelievable!" marveled Joe. "It really
helped, kid. Without it, we'd be all be dead or
drained by now."

"But KRON got away."

"Yes, but we think we've trapped it at last. And
the time has come to make our move, so I'm here to
ask you to volunteer for a dangerous mission."

Suddenly the condor spoke. "Young man," she
said to Paul, "I'm going to give you a piece of
advice. Of course, nobody ever listens to *me.*" She
paused and rotated her homely head cautiously
toward Joe and back to Paul before she croaked:
"Never hurry. Never worry. NEVER VOLUNTEER."

"I'm sorry to hear you say that, ma'am," said Joe,
"because we hoped you would go, too. Your com-
manding eagle recommends you both for the mission. She says nobody else can fly like you."

"That's true," said Paul eagerly.

For a moment the condor puffed up like a turkey gobbler, and then she let her feathers settle slowly back in place.

"Oh, well, whatever will be, will be," she said. "If this young man needs me, I'll go. Oh, yes, do or die. That's the way I am."

She objected loudly to the idea of carrying Joe too, but eventually, after more flattery and persuasion, she consented to the whole plan, which Joe explained as they flew toward KRON's stronghold.

Joe seemed much older and more confident than the wounded soldier Paul had met in the forest — was it only that morning? How could it be? But he must stop wondering about that and pay attention to instructions.

"This is a commando raid," Joe told them, "and we're attacking at dusk just before they turn on their night vision equipment. We must land in exactly the right place (which is where we need you, ma'am) to draw them out of their dens and destroy them. There! Right there! Straight down! Ready, kid?"

With Paul controlling the jet on the survival knife, the condor executed a perfect two-point landing in the shadow of a big rock.

Paul couldn't help giving her a hug that raised lots of dust from her feathers and made them both cough. Then she took off, paused for a moment to dip one wing in a final salute, and hid herself in the deepening twilight of the sky while Joe and Paul began their risky mission. First they planted a series of small explosives that were intended more to attract attention than to do damage.

"Will this really bring them out?" asked Paul.

"Enough of 'em."

"But we want all of them. We want KRON."

"It'll come."

"How can you be sure?"

Joe paused for a moment before he answered. "It'll come because of us."

"What do you mean?"

"Ever since the ambush and the bomb, it's holding a grudge, and more than anything else, it wants me and you. Especially you."

"Why?" said Paul, but in his heart he knew why.

"Because you made it. When you first told me that, I didn't understand. But now I do. If you make it, you own it. You're just a kid, but you have special powers. As long as you've still got your brain, the thing called KRON is incomplete. Unfinished. Kind of soft. And you've got some control over it, in spite of all the other brains it's sucked up. Even now, almost beaten, KRON is still very dangerous. Because . . . if it could suck your mind away from you, KRON and KRON alone would be supreme."

Paul understood. He was the worm on the hook. He was taking the gravest of risks, but at the same time, he himself was a terrible threat — to the Greens as well as to KRON. If KRON caught him, he,

Cliff

Paul, would become the ultimate monster. That was his own special danger, and that led to a special responsibility.

It was almost too dark to see when, with shaky fingers, he lighted the first fuse, and he and Joe took cover behind a boulder.

Boom!

Paul wished that he still had his earplugs. He wished that he were at home in his comfortable bed. He even wished that he were sitting safe and bored at his desk in school — even if it meant practicing his handwriting.

Boom! Boom! Boom!

Now the Drainers were coming; he could hear them clambering from their subterranean hideouts. Now, if all went well, the Green forces would arrive to hammer them from ground and air. And for a while everything did go well; several waves of Drainers were successfully squelched, and when a lull came, Joe and Paul raced to another location and planted more decoy explosives, this time not far from the brink of one of the great cliffs.

But when they had hidden again, Paul whispered, "Is KRON really down there?"

"As far as we know. Why?"

Paul laid his ear against the rocks. "I don't hear anything."

"What would you hear?"

"My Voice."

Maybe he did hear it: the faintest of maddening

repeated sounds. Paul concentrated hard and tried again, but this time he heard nothing.

Joe was puzzled. "Your own voice?" he said.

"No, no," whispered Paul. "KRON's, I think. In a way."

"But KRON is silent."

"Not to me. Shh!"

Now Paul did hear something, but it was the slow, calm talk of the rocks. He pressed himself against them and strained his ears to catch their message.

"Be . . . "

"You aren't much help," said Paul. "Be what?"

"Be . . . neath. Be . . . low. Be . . . hind."

"Could this be a warning?" he thought.

"BE . . . WARE!" said the rocks.

At the same moment Joe elbowed him. "Drainers!"

Killercrawlers like hideous oversized tarantulas came surging over the ridge behind them, and Paul saw that the tip of each armored tentacle was a micropump. He could almost feel the suction, and the Greens were nowhere in sight. The only alternatives left for Joe and Paul seemed to be capture . . . or the cliff.

Or perhaps a third. Paul reached for his survival knife and fanned out the blades and attachments, searching among them for something he hadn't yet tried. When this was all over, he thought, he would ask Joe if he'd known about the fantastic powers

Cliff

the knife possessed when he gave it away.

"No time now," Paul told himself as his fingers closed around the long thin tube. Maybe the flame-shaped button would operate it, too, he thought, and he pressed it. Instantly a gorgeous orange plume of real fire bloomed from the tube and engulfed the closest killercrawler, first withering its tentacles and then melting and toasting the crawler like a marshmallow. A horde of gray Braindrainers leaped from it, flaming before they melted too.

But more Drainers poured in behind the first ones. Paul flamed them while Joe lobbed his little explosives into the conflagration with his one good hand. Like all fires, this one was a beautiful and terrible sight, but the twisting, dissolving figures of the Drainers and the killercrawlers made it the most horrible bonfire Paul ever witnessed.

The invasion was now proving to be a major Braindrainer offensive; they poured from the rocks like angry ants, and the faster Paul burned them, the faster they came — too many to hold back with just one flame. And Joe had run out of explosives.

In desperation Paul shouted: "Rocks! Is KRON down there with you? Don't just sit there and erode. Do something! Rumble! Shake! Quake!"

And they did. Great shudders ran through the mountain, and it shrugged the Drainers off like flies. Their tunnels collapsed; their killercrawlers tumbled thousands of feet to their doom. The earthquake was a mixed blessing, however, since it not only wrecked the Drainers and their stronghold, but it also remodeled the geography of the mountain range, tilting the top and sending Paul and Joe slipping toward the edge of the cliff.

"The grappling hook!" thought Paul, frantically reaching for his survival knife. But how could one hook save them both? What about the jet? But how could they fly without wings?

At that instant, just as they began to lose their grips and skidded closer and closer to the deathly precipice, Paul saw the scissors and remembered his bulletproof vest. He ripped it off, and within a few feverish seconds he had cut out a pair of paper shapes that resembled a block letter Y.

Cliff

He folded one arm of each Y forward, and the other arm backward.

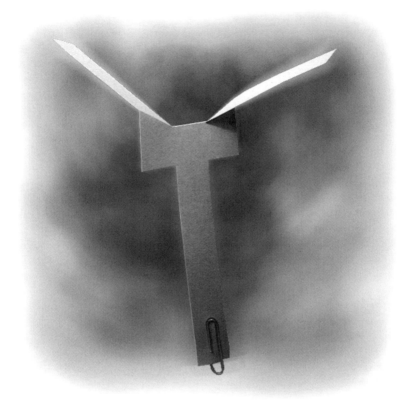

And then he handed one of the devices to Joe, who gasped, "Are you crazy? What is this?"

"Grab the bottom and hold on tight," Paul told

him. Ordinarily he would add paper clips for the
necessary ballast, but in a pinch like this, the weight
of their bodies would serve just as well.

"But — but — "

"It's a helicopter!"

And together they leaped into space.

Cliff

Saturn

"Yes, he *is* here! Oh, thank heavens!"

Wrapped in a strange trance, Paul heard his mother's voice and struggled to open his eyes and move his arms and legs, which were heavy, stiff, and chilly, like the limbs of a mannequin. And once his eyes were open, he did not understand why everything around him was still dark, except for the flashlight in his mother's hand. Ouch! He covered his eyes with his fingers, for the light struck like a blow.

"Wake up, Paul," Mom said.

He could tell that she was working to keep her voice quiet and level. What had he done? Where was he? It was not the middle of the night, for filmy orange traces of sunset still streaked the western sky. Then he recognized the floor of the tree fort, and the adventures of the afternoon started to trickle back into his memory. He must have landed safely here, but where was Joe?

"That's right, sit up," Mom said, putting her arm

around him. It felt especially good because he was cold. "We couldn't find you in your room, or the rest of the house, and you didn't answer when we called. Your dad and I got worried."

"We thought you'd flown the coop," said Dad from the bottom of the ladder.

From his father's joking tone, Paul knew that in spite of disobeying instructions and frightening his parents, he was, miraculously, not in trouble at all. At least, not at the moment.

"*I* noticed your window was open," added Katie's voice, also from the darkness below the tree.

Mom shone her flashlight around the tree fort, revealing the open ammunition box, the empty army canteen, a popped balloon, many burned-out matches, and several little puddles of scorched gray plastic.

"Paul, it's dangerous to light fires in the tree house — " she began, then bit off the sentence in the middle. "Time to go inside," she said, more cheerfully. "Let's see what we can do about that temperature of yours."

She guided Paul's legs over the edge of the tree fort, and Dad helped his toes find the rungs of the ladder. Two tiny pin-prick stars and a bright coppery planet now gleamed overhead, almost as though they had been hung in the tree as decorations. To Paul's watering eyes the house with its windows all aglow in the night looked like a home in a faraway country: perhaps some fairy-tale cottage in the dark woods, in an old oil painting in a hushed museum. This house surely belonged to some other family, and he could never, never go inside. Yet he did.

Once inside, stumbling toward his bedroom, he overheard his mother say the word "delirious," followed by a question that included the word "emergency." His father went to the telephone and called Paul's and Katie's doctor. None of this seemed particularly interesting to Paul, who was taking readings on himself.

"I've never felt so many different ways in one day," he thought. "High and low, giant and miniature, scared and safe . . ."

At the moment he felt oddly transparent. Little shivers ran across the skin of his back, as though it were made of water. His mother opened his bedroom door for him, and even Paul could see that the room was a mess. The pattern on his wallpaper appeared to be throbbing in time with his head. Afraid of KRON and the Voice, he hesitated to go inside. But Mom smoothed his bed and tucked him in, and after a while Dad came and stood in the doorway.

"Since the fever is his only symptom, the doctor says there's not much we can do except try to lower it. Sunset is fever time, he says. But if Paul's temperature stays high much longer, we should take him to the clinic."

Something cool and moist touched Paul's throbbing forehead.

Saturn

"We'll try this first," his mother said.

Her fingers touched his skin like icicles as she sponged his face and neck with water. Then she brought cool drinks for slow sipping, ice chips for sucking, and medicine. After a while, Paul's headache loosened its grip on his skull, and his wallpaper came into normal focus again.

"It's down!" reported his mother, reading the thermometer with a smile of relief.

"Mom," he said, "what exactly is a virus?"

"A very tiny particle," she said. "Even smaller than a cell. Viruses make you sick by moving into your cells and growing there, like parasites."

Some people believed viruses were alive, she explained, and others disagreed, saying that they only stole life from their victims.

"What do they look like?" asked Paul.

"Some look like threads, and others are odd geometrical shapes — rods and balls and round heads with tails, like comets. Don't worry, Paul. I think yours is almost beaten now."

Even so, nothing sounded good to eat, so he refused dinner and lay quietly listening to the distant clinks and clatters of the family meal, finding the sounds reassuring. It was good to be home with his family nearby.

"Dang!" he said to himself. "War sure wears you out."

Now he supposed it was all over; his new friends and his enemies were equally distant. He could only

THE BOY WITH PAPER WINGS

vaguely remember the helicopter ride, the sensation of spinning and falling, spinning and falling almost forever.

Skree-ee-eek, went the branch against the window-pane.

When he tumbled at last into the trees, they had turned themselves marvelously soft to make a safe landing for him and Joe. And now that he came to think about it, Paul guessed that the trees had recognized their friends and relations in the paper of the helicopters. Every piece of paper must contain the ghosts of many trees, he thought. Through his uncurtained window he saw the zigzag network of branches outlined against the sky, and above them a sparkling profusion of stars and planets. Except for them, the night was unusually dark, for the moon would not rise till late.

His own phosphorescent constellations glowed on the ceiling, and as he lay in bed and gazed at them he realized that he was definitely feeling better. And he had an idea. What if he made an airplane from glow-in-the-dark paper? Even better, why not make a spacecraft — a spectacular, luminous starship? The effect would be truly awesome if he flew it off the roof in the dark. Paul turned on his bedside lamp and sat up, excited, but there was one problem: he had no phosphorescent paper, and he didn't even know where to buy it. Perhaps regular paper could be painted.

"Yes," thought Paul. "I really need some

Saturn   139

luminous paint. Think of the dioramas I could make!"

Just for tonight, though, he must use a rectangle of plain paper.

"Plain — plane — planet," he murmured as he started to fold. "That's it, a planet plane. Let's see, what shall I call you? I know! This mono-wing looks like a ring . . . a wing ring for a planet plane . . . so your name is — *Saturn!*"

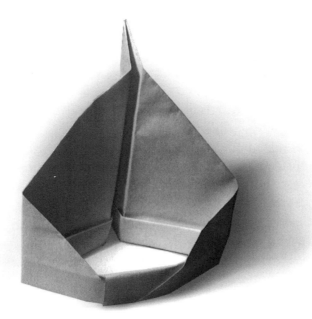

He had often wished for a planet of his very own, a world exactly to his taste, and he always thought that clouds made of whipped cream would be an excellent way to start. Then, down below, there must be an infinite supply of hot fudge sundaes and pumpkin pie. And what else? Well, friends. Games. Answers to questions. Stories of superheroes. Mom and Dad would visit quite often. He wasn't sure about Katie.

"And I would have a workshop," he said to himself. "One with all the tools and supplies I would ever need, just floating into my hands at the right moment."

Of course, on his very own perfect planet he would be able to fly, effortlessly, anytime and anywhere he liked. Once, when he was imagining this ideal planet of his, he had asked Katie what she would like to have on hers.

"Lots of places to turn cartwheels!" she said promptly.

"Is that all?"

"And then, let's see . . . well, nobody would ever cry or get sick or die, and whenever you wanted anything, you would just say, 'Be!' and it would happen."

He had to admit that some of Katie's ideas were good. Perhaps he would let her visit his planet now and then.

He poised the finished Saturn in his palm and started the countdown.

"Three . . . two . . . one . . . liftoff!"

But it was much harder than he'd thought it would be to blast into space. First came an

Saturn

overpowering rumble, followed by nearly unbearable pressure and dizziness, and through it all, the Saturn proved quite tricky to fly; at first Paul found himself soaring upside down and backwards.

"Even though there's no up and no down in space," he thought, "there is such a thing as navigation, and I'm not doing it. Help!"

But eventually he mastered the spacecraft, and they left the pretty little Earth far behind and headed for the outer planets. As they cruised across the solar system, Paul felt rather bored with all the same old stops, those well-known tourist attractions of Mars, Jupiter, Saturn, Uranus, and even distant Neptune. Most of the giant planets that they passed were shrouded in nasty clouds of methane or ammonia gas.

"I wouldn't bother with them," thought Paul, peering through the porthole, "unless those clouds were whipped cream!"

He did feel a certain interest in Pluto. Perhaps he would stop there. But Paul was much more intrigued by the notion that there still might be an undiscovered Planet X beyond Pluto in the most distant orbit of all. Maybe he would be the one to find Planet X. Maybe then he could name it Planet P! At any rate, it wouldn't do any harm to look.

When they approached Pluto, it looked so fearfully cold and uninviting that Paul chose not to land after all. He should have worn his jacket, he thought, for somehow, in spite of the fever burning inside him, he had never felt really warm since his nap in the tree fort.

"If there really is a Planet X," he said to himself, shivering, "I hope it's like Hawaii!"

But now vast volumes of space opened out in front of the Saturn without the slightest sign of Planet X, or anyplace else for Paul to land. At unimaginable distances he saw infinitesimal points of light.

"Probably from stars that are already dead," Paul thought, suddenly full of loneliness and gloom and a tiny itchy foreboding of disaster, and he wondered if he should turn back.

But then he remembered Katie's suggestion, and he decided to try it. He leaned forward and spoke clearly into space.

"Be!" he said.

And there it was.

Saturn

Flats

Planet X was small, like
one of the moons of Mars,
but it had a much more
attractive and mysterious appearance than chunky
little Phobos and Deimos. X was perfectly spherical,
and its surface seemed to be smooth and the color
of ivory. It cast a glow upon the endless night of
space, as though it carried some source of light
inside itself, and it was crisscrossed with many fine
black lines like cracks or squiggles.

"Or scribbles," thought Paul in great excitement,
steering the Saturn closer to the mystery planet. "Or
even canals!"

Of course he knew that the idea of canals on
Mars had turned out to be mistaken, but that didn't
mean that other planets might not have them — or
have intelligent life, either. If he had learned one
single thing during this long day, it was what the
albatross had told him: that the universe contained
worlds within worlds. The question was, how did
they all fit together? Was it like Katie's Russian doll,

a series of nested objects? Was his Sunday school teacher right when she suggested that, for all we knew, the solar system was an atom in God's footstool?

"But why would God need a footstool?" thought Paul.

Mom would say that anything that the human brain could imagine was possible, in one way or another; and Dad would say that the answer to the universe question was "PHYSICS," but at the moment they weren't there to explain further. Once Paul had read that space was curved: now *that* was an interesting idea! And he had heard also that long ago the universe began with a Big Bang, and it was still expanding after that great explosion, which would eventually be followed by a Big Crunch. Ouch! Paul wondered if Scout ever puzzled over such problems, but the contents of that little black cat head were, in their own way, as remote as the farthest star.

Soon the Saturn would land, and then perhaps Paul would discover some answers on his own. He began to feel the gravitational pull of Planet X, which was unlike any sensation he had experienced before. It left him as breathless as an asthma attack. This was very strange, he thought, because such a small planet ought to have a weak gravitational field. He clutched uselessly at his chest, his throat, his nose, and his eyes, for some terrible force seemed to be crushing his head. Through the pain, he sensed the approach of total collapse, and sure enough the Saturn, too, began to crackle, unfold, and flatten.

There was no time to be afraid. Like a sheet of newspaper in a stiff breeze, the surface of the planet blew upward to meet him. For one long instant Paul watched the curious lines overlap into many little black X's, and then with a tremendous slap he landed.

Silence. Stillness. Whiteness. Nothingness.

But not quite. After a while, he saw a single dark dot, and then another. First they stood still, and then they drifted closer to him. Next, a fine black line came into focus, followed by a crooked one that angled its way up to his face. And then more dots appeared. It was like watching mysterious patterns form on a computer screen.

"I think I can think," said Paul to himself. "But I can't move."

He felt most peculiar. He existed, all right, but he seemed to lack all substance, depth, and weight.

Tiny sparkles of meaning crept into his mind, not nearly as loud as the rock talk or even the whispers of trees; in fact there was no sound at all, and not a single word, but simply meaning.

The first message was a question, which seemed to rise from one of the dots: "What is it?"

"Well, it's certainly not straight," replied the zigzag line. "It wanders all around, and then finally it reconnects to itself. So it must be some kind of

Flats

simple closed curve. I've never seen anything quite like it."

"Whatever it is, it's a very irregular body," added the straight line disdainfully, and the dots giggled.

Paul felt rather insulted. He decided to try to communicate with these creatures by directing his thoughts in their direction. "Hey," he thought to them, "I'm *almost* symmetrical. I have two of most things, and the rest are usually centered."

The lines as well as the dots found this very funny. Their laughter tingled and tickled inside Paul's brain like gnats crawling over his thoughts.

"Who are you? What is this place?" he asked.

Answers came from all directions, and they were all the same mathematical expression: "= X."

"So this *is* Planet X!" said Paul.

"X = X," they repeated, with more giggles.

"Why can't I stand up and walk around?"

"What an absurd idea!" cried the straight line.

"I don't like it at all," muttered a square.

"What is 'stand up'?" asked a dot.

"X is a flat plane, not a planet (whatever that may be)," said the crooked line importantly, "and it is inhabited by points, lines, and two-dimensional figures such as you, Simple Closed Curve."

"Two dimensions! But I have three dimensions!"

The little dots, which Paul now realized were actually points, lined up in a row around his head, forming a semicircle, and then they all squeaked together: "No, you don't!"

And suddenly Paul saw that they were right. Somehow, possibly from the unusual gravity of Planet X, or the impact of landing, or some other cause that he did not understand, he had become entirely flat — no more than the outline of a boy upon a piece of paper. And speaking of paper, the former Saturn lay not far away from him: a neat rectangle measuring 8½ by 11 inches.

Soon the word spread, and many other inhabitants of the plane of Planet X came to stand and gawk, including a horde of squares and their various four-sided cousins, a collection of different types of triangles, and a multitude of other polygons — pentagons, hexagons, octagons, and so forth. The circles arrived last and stayed only briefly before they whirled away again, apparently bored.

"They think they're better than the rest of us," whispered a friendly triangle. "But really there's no reason for them to be such snobs. We triangles are every bit as complicated and important as those dizzy circles."

The points floated by in crowds, like dust, while most of the lines never stopped at all, but passed through like freight trains.

"They go on forever, you know," explained the triangle, which had settled down next to Paul's left ear. It was a medium-sized equilateral triangle about the size of the palm of Paul's hand.

"But where do the lines go?"

"Does it matter?"

Flats

"Well, maybe not," said Paul, struggling hard against his flatness, but failing to rise above it. "Oh, *fishcakes!* I wish I could get back to my old self again. There's a whole other dimension, you know, that's called space, and then there's time, which makes four, and beyond that, who knows? Maybe there are even more."

The triangle moved a little closer. "Yes, I've heard these rumors," it murmured. "But it's all very hard to imagine, and possibly wicked. Don't talk too loud."

"Will I be stuck here forever?" Paul wondered.

He remembered his survival knife, but there was no way to reach it, and even if he could, it was probably reduced to a mere outline, too. Then he thought of the Saturn, and the Eagle, and the Manta Ray, and the Lifeboat, and the Owl, and he tried something new: "Fold!" he said to himself, and he made a mighty effort.

At first it seemed that nothing had happened. And then far away at the edge of the universe, just for an instant, he heard his mother's voice calling him.

"Paul! Paul!"

And Paul sat up. He was still very flat, hardly more than a paper doll, but at least he was able to move, and he had gained some slight thickness. He listened carefully, but Mom's voice did not call again, and there was no other sign of her anywhere. The triangle, meanwhile, was extremely impressed.

"Extraordinary!" it cried. "Remarkable! But now I can only see two little bits of you. Come back, Simple Closed Curve! Talk to me! Can I come too?"

Paul was feeling up his sleeve for his knife, which he was overjoyed to find there, for he had a hunch he would need it soon. From his new perspective, the plane of Planet X looked like an enormous sheet of scratch paper, all covered with the diagrams and doodles of some gigantic mathematician. At his feet lay his new friend the triangle, glowing a little with excitement, and calling, "Take me with you! I want to go, too!"

"I'm not sure how to do that," said Paul. "If I cut you out with my little scissors, you would still be flat."

"Cut me out?" said the triangle doubtfully.

"Like this," said Paul. He chose a long, thin rectangle out of the two-dimensional crowd below and ran the scissors all around it.

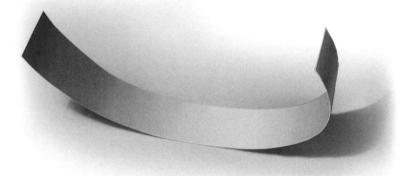

As he lifted it up, he suddenly remembered a way to give the strip a three-dimensional shape, even though it had only one side and one edge. It was a paper trick that his father had once showed him. He gave the strip a half-twist and pinched the two ends together.

"Look," he said. "It's a Möbius strip. I can run my finger from any point to any other point without ever crossing over the edge. And if I cut it along the center, parallel to the edge, it stays in one piece even though it's divided in half. Very cool."

"EEK!" said the strip. "Help! That tickles!"

At this, some of the other squiggles and scribbles became agitated.

"Danger! Danger!" cried the points.

"It's strange, much too strange, and it ought to be against the law," grumbled the lines.

"It's kidnapping!" cried the other rectangles.

To reassure them, Paul untwisted the strip and fitted it back into its place, and lay down flat again

Flats

himself, finding the plane as cool and comfortable as a sheet in a bed. For an instant he wondered if it was really worth all the trouble to stand up again and try to return to his normal round self. And even if he could, how would he ever get home without his spaceship? Could he remember how to fold the Saturn again?

Then the triangle scooted close to his ear again and whispered, "Don't mind them. They're awfully narrow minded, really."

"I think I know how to bring you with me," Paul said. "I kind of saw it in my head. Do you still want to come?"

The triangle bravely said yes, so Paul rose up again and began the triangle's transformation.

Polys

First he cut out the triangle.

Then he folded each cor-
ner toward the middle so
that all three points met at the top of the shape.

And what was once a two-dimensional triangle,
or flat polygon, became a perfect three-dimensional
pyramid with four separate triangular faces — a
solid little polyhedron.

"Ah!" it cried, sitting up amazed in Paul's hand.
Besides four faces, it now had four voices, which
sounded in unison, like a quartet of singers.

"Amazing — amazing — amazing — amazing!"

If Paul had made the pyramid at home, he would
have glued or taped the edges together, but in this
strange third dimension of Planet X, there was
apparently no need for glue or tape. The edges simply grew together. And then the pyramid expanded
rapidly and evenly in every direction until it was a
little taller than Paul, as they protruded into space
side by side.

"Is this all — all — all — all?" hummed the

THE BOY WITH PAPER WINGS

pyramid's four voices, looking around. The immediate area was empty except for the two of them. Off at a distance, through wisps of mist (not a bit like whipped cream, unfortunately) Paul thought he could see other solid shapes resembling mountains, or perhaps the skyscrapers of a great city of glass. Down on the plane he noticed an outline shaped like a cross, four equal squares long and three across.

Once more in his mind's eye he saw solid possibilities in the flat shape. Inside Paul's head, the figure folded up like a cardboard box, and he saw exactly how to make it with his hands. Bending over, he cut it out, and then he folded the squares toward one another. It would be another polyhedron.

Polys

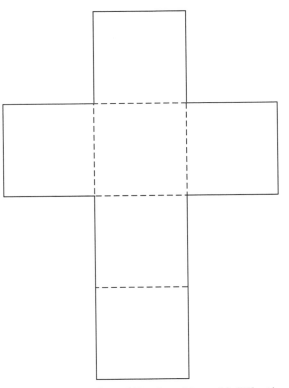

"Poly, poly . . . " said Paul to himself. "That's what I'll call them! They're the Polys!"

When the new Poly was finished, it also grew larger and stood on its own. Then he introduced it to the pyramid: "This," he said, "is a cube."

"Properly speaking, a hexahedron," corrected the cube, in a superior tone. "And *you*," it said, turning to the pyramid, "are a *tetra*hedron. I have six sides, while you have only four."

Each of the six square faces also possessed its own voice, and harmonizing together they made a little choir. Each sound rang out six times simultaneously, and the music wrapped all around Paul and created new dimensions in his ears. Proudly the cube rolled itself over and over to show off its sides, like a die in a game of chance.

"Well, we're both perfectly regular," said the pyramid stoutly. "Each of our sides is exactly the same as the rest. We are crystals. We are jewels."

"We are magnificent," agreed the cube's six voices.

"Just wait!" said Paul. "I see another one of you down there!"

Polys

The next Poly pattern that he snipped from the plane was an arrangement of eight triangles, like a snake with its head raised:

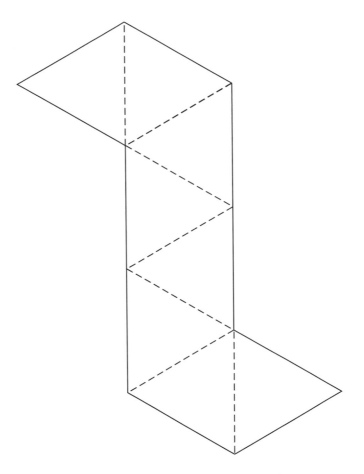

And he folded it into an eight-sided Poly, or octahedron.

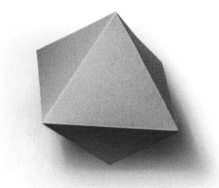

"You look a little like both of us," observed the cube to the octahedron.

"It's me, doubled!" said the pyramid.

"Not exactly," chorused the eight faces of the octahedron, each one glittering in the pearly light reflected from the surface of Planet X. "I am my very own exquisite self — self — self — "

"Yes, yes," interrupted the pyramid. "Lovely, lovely, et cetera, et cetera. Is that all?" it asked again, nudging Paul.

"Not quite," he said. Another method to turn a flat Poly into a solid Poly had blossomed in his head: this time he cut out a pattern that looked like two flowers, touching. Each one was composed of five petals and a center, and each petal and center was a pentagon.

"Ooh, what can it be?" sang out the pyramid, the cube, and the octahedron in their eighteen voices.

This Poly was somewhat more difficult to fold,

Polys

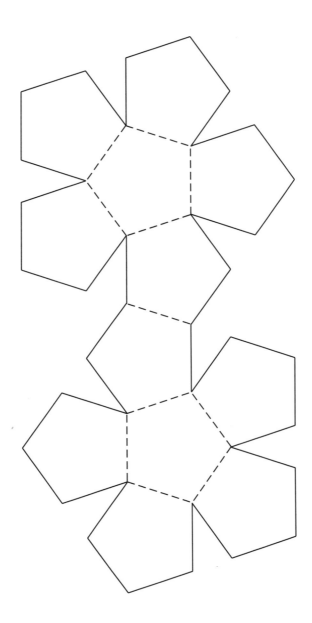

THE BOY WITH PAPER WINGS

but at last Paul's fingers turned the two flowers into a twelve-sided ball, or dodecahedron.

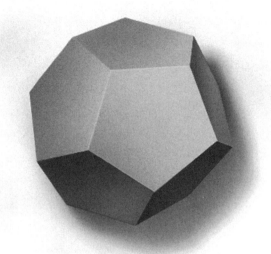

"Twelve! Just imagine!" said the pyramid, awestruck. "Does this go on forever — ever — ever — ever?"

"No," answered Paul, who was beginning to feel tired and dizzy. "I mean, there are lots of other shapes, but I think they're all irregular, like me, or else they're rounded shapes like cones and spheres. Maybe there might be one more Poly with straight equal sides. Let me see . . ."

This time he had to concentrate all his attention on the problem and to look long and hard across the plane before he visualized the design: five rows of four equilateral triangles.

Polys

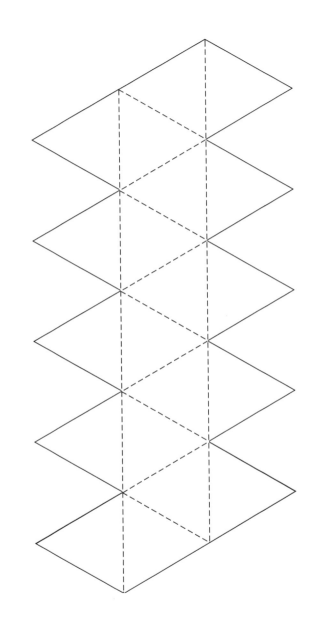

THE BOY WITH PAPER WINGS

As the tiny survival scissors slashed around its zigzag edges, he wondered what he would do when he was finished making polyhedrons. Could there be yet another level, or dimension, of folding? He tried to imagine what it might be. And at that moment Paul noticed trouble brewing on the plane: all of the flat shapes, lines, curves, and points were seething like black noodles in boiling soup. As quickly as he could, he bent the strip of triangles into a loop and folded all the points until they all met at top and bottom, producing something with twenty equal sides, rather like a soccer ball.

"What are you?" cried the other Polys.

The answer came back in a fine surge of sound, twenty voices from twenty spinning

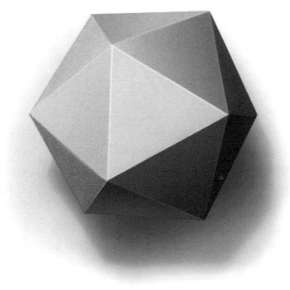

Polys

faces: "I-CO-SA-HE-DRON."

"Beautiful," the others cooed. "Perfect. Exquisite. Just like us!"

And as the icosahedron continued its song, the other Polys joined in.

Amazing space
How great the sound
That raised
A scrap like me . . .

Listening, half hypnotized by all this harmony, Paul forgot about the geometry soup. Instead he wondered again about the next step in folding. What if he started with a polyhedron, and folded *it* up? What sort of shape, in what sort of dimension, would come into being?

"I once was flat," crooned the Polys, "but now am round . . ."

"Yes!" thought Paul. What would happen if you made an arrangement of cubes, like a cross, and folded up the arms . . . But then the idea slipped away from him, and he let out a yelp of pain.

"Ouch! Hey, stop it! That hurts!" said Paul.

The points ground into his heels and toes like grains of broken glass. The lines pricked his feet like needles. The curves hooked him like little sharp horns. The other flat shapes jostled and bashed him, too, and every single one of them screamed "No! No! No!" at such a high pitch and so steadily that his skull vibrated and his thoughts became deformed.

To his horror, he felt himself flattening again.

Very, very far away, Dad said: "Paul? Look at me. Paul?"

But much closer, right inside his head along with all the screams, he heard something else.

Na na na. Na na na na.

"I *knew* KRON wasn't inside the mountain," thought Paul. But there wasn't much consolation in being right, for the last battle remained to be fought.

"I can't stay here," Paul told the five Polys, which broke off their song and fluttered doubtfully in space like asteroids that had lost their way. "You can stay, if you want to go back down to the plane and flatten into triangles, or squares, or pentagons again. Or you can hang in space. But I must go."

"How?" he wondered privately. "And where?"

However and wherever he went, he must quiet the Voice, and he must find KRON. It was inevitable. This was the moment of truth, probably his last chance to conquer KRON, and perhaps also his last chance to find his way home again. Yet he felt cool and peaceful, light and clever and incredibly deft.

Na na na.

He summoned up all his power, paper-thin as he was, and every last particle of his Paulness, which was, he realized, something just as unique as triangularity or roundness, and he shouted mightily: "Fold!"

Like a paper airplane, he folded himself a pair of

wings, a fuselage, and a tail. And then somewhere he found the strength to give one last command: "Fly!"

And he flew.

Home

It was the flight of his life.
It was infinitely more wonderful than any of the ear-
lier ones, for now Paul was pilot and plane, lift and
thrust, matter and energy all in one. After a little
while, he realized that the five Polys had decided to
come, too, for he heard their fifty voices chanting.

Fire, air
All share
Water, earth
Death, birth
Spheres turn
Stars burn
Hero
Zero . . .
Fly, fly, fly, fly, fly!

And together they flew almost forever.

With a dip of his wings or nose or tail, Paul could
perform any maneuver he wished. It was better than
his dreams . . . except that space was dark and

mostly blank, and he'd always dreamed of flying through blue sky and white clouds. He felt completely free . . . except for the vague sense of doom hanging over him. And after a while, Paul noticed that although they had traveled farther than he could imagine, they had come no closer to home, or to KRON.

Then it spoke: *Na na na NA na.*

And the infuriating Voice continued to call to him but always stayed some distance away, as though Paul were It in a game of blindman's buff.

Perhaps, thought Paul as he chased and dodged without success, this terrible mindless game would go on forever. Perhaps *that* would be KRON's triumph. Worried and distracted, he forgot to look where he was going, and so he burst without warning from the darkness of space into a glowing spectrum of colors.

"Gosh," gasped Paul. "It's the biggest rainbow I ever saw!"

It contained all the iridescence of bubbles and feathers and mother-of-pearl, but it was more than that, too. Soundless, tasteless, without substance, texture, or smell, coiled into the shape of a snail, the mysterious spectrum threw its colors over Paul's white paper self, and as it did, it soaked him with thoughts.

Later, he could only remember a few of them, including dragons, sword blades, sweet peas in bloom, birthday cakes, caterpillars, diamonds,

intricate engines, Christmas Eve, summer rain-
storms, neon signs, computer circuits, new shoes,
and soft, shifting sand.

"Who are you?" Paul breathed.

And it answered in light and colors, without
words: "I am the Space Worm."

"Space Worm?"

Paul couldn't help laughing, but the Space Worm
didn't seem to mind. It calmly continued to glow.

"Before you can come to terms with KRON," it
said (without speaking), "you must learn to understand the Voice."

"But it never says anything except *na na na!*"

"Listen."

And this time, sure enough, Paul caught the
meaning of the drone: "You'll never go home, never
go home, never go home. You're in my power now."

"What?" cried Paul.

"Keep listening."

"You're in my power now. You're in my universe
now."

"What does it mean?"

"Look. Think."

Still at a distance, the blue-and-green clay figure
of KRON became visible, writhing incessantly from
one grotesque shape to another.

"You're in another space, another time. Your
family's dust, your home is lost and gone. You're in
my power now," droned KRON.

"Is that true?" demanded Paul.

Home

Gradually and gracefully the Worm began to uncoil itself, and Paul saw that it possessed something like a head on each end. A different message came from each head.

"Yes," said one end of the Space Worm.

"No!" yelled Paul.

"No," said the other.

"Stop it!" Paul roared. "And explain!"

Fully unrolled, the Space Worm was extremely long, so that its two heads melted away into the distance and stopped contradicting each other while the whole Worm radiated at Paul, red and green, yellow and purple, blue and orange messages. Both heads turned out to be correct, however: Paul *was* in another space and time. For when he had folded himself to escape Planet X, Paul had rocketed out of his own universe and flown into another, a feat that required tremendous energy.

"You can't go home again," taunted KRON. "You've used up all your power. You're nothing but paper now. You'd burn to ashes in a millisecond. You might as well stay with me. Join me! Be me! Together we can control anything we like, blow up whatever we please, and fly anytime!"

At this, the rainbow colors grew a little brighter, like a fire that has been breathed upon. "I am the Space Worm. I chew the wormholes that connect one universe with another. Now that you understand, don't listen to KRON. Think for yourself. Think. Think."

The great Worm spiraled away from him and disappeared, and Paul caught a glimpse of the hole it left behind. Down, down, down it went, and where did it end? At least KRON was something he knew, and power was something he liked. But the decision was really very simple, after all.

"It's better to create," Paul said to himself, "than to destroy."

Just as he launched himself through the opening of the wormhole, he discovered that now he had hands again, so he grabbed at the place where KRON still hovered.

"You come too!" growled Paul.

He caught KRON! Then he lost him.

And Paul began to fall.

"Bye, Polys!" he called over his shoulder.

"Bye-bye . . . " they answered, their voices chiming like bells.

Down, down, down. To Paul's surprise the wormhole was rather bare and drab and full of echoes, like a back stairway in a tall building. Dust, mixed with the smell of machine oil, made his nose sting, and once he thought he glimpsed some buckets and a large, grimy mop. Then, suddenly, as though her lips were at his ear, he heard his mother say, "Paul, wake up."

"No, no," he wanted to tell her. "Everything's under control. Everything's glorious. I'm in hyperspace!"

But he could not stop to talk because he had

Home

burst from the wormhole and was flying from dimension to dimension. There were many, many more of these than he had ever imagined, and they branched off at perpendicular angles from each another to form an astonishing jungle gym of possibilities.

And universe after universe ran parallel to one another, stacked like sheets of paper or exquisite crystals, full of shapes, colors, sounds, smells, and textures. Paul tried to memorize bits of the structure as he navigated through this kaleidoscope, but the designs slithered in and out of his mind just as KRON had slipped and slithered through his fingers.

"It's a city made of pictures, on top of music, on top of math," he thought. "It's a computer . . . a brain."

But it did not last.

Na na na na.

KRON was on the loose in hyperspace, surrounded by a flock of winged Drainers.

"This time I'm going to get you!" Paul swore.

He pulled out the survival knife, wondering if any of the attachments could possibly help him now. Paul slashed at the clay figure with the laser blade, but KRON only laughed.

NA na na na na.

Meanwhile, the Drainers closed in on Paul.

"Maybe I can use the jet to blow them away from me," he thought, locating the nozzle and aiming it at the enemies all around him. KRON and the

Drainers had gotten into his own bedroom, and they hung over his bed, mixed up with flashing lights and stars.

"I know!" he thought. "I'll reverse the jet!"

"Whoa, boy," said his father's voice, and big hands seized him and held him gently.

A powerful suction roared from the nozzle and caught up the Drainers like a vacuum cleaner. Then Paul got his hands on KRON and crushed him.

"Whoa!" said Dad again.

The multiple dimensions and universes, the enemies, and the geometric figures all collapsed and vanished. The old familiar world returned in full force, round and real and darkly shadowed; it was the middle of the night.

"What's happening?" asked Katie sleepily.

"It's the fever again," said his mother with a catch in her voice.

Paul recognized her flannel nightgown, his father's brown bathrobe, Katie's startled face in the doorway, and Scout perched on top of the bookcase like a black owl with a long electric tail.

"But he's not hot," said Dad. "He's sweating a little, but his skin feels cool. He's much better."

Mom knelt down to see for herself, stroking Paul's hair away from his forehead and smiling at him.

"It was just a dream," she said.

Paul wanted to tell her no, it was not, but he felt too tired to talk. He looked down and saw that the

Home

bed was littered with paper scraps, and in his trembling hands the blue-and-green figure was no longer recognizable, for he had just pummeled it into a greasy ball of modeling clay.

Paul released a great, long sigh.

"Tomorrow," he thought, "I'll mold it into something absolutely new."

Suggestions for Further Exploration

Computer Software

The Greatest Paper Airplanes. Software for both Macintosh and IBM computers, Kittyhawk Software, Inc., P. O. Box 64189, Tucson, Arizona 85728 (800-777-5745). (Animated, three-dimensional folding directions for fifty airplanes, including Owl, Albatross, Manta Ray, Eagle, Condor, and Saturn.)

Books

Abbott, Edwin A. *Flatland: A Romance of Many Dimensions.* London, 1884. (Available in many editions.)

Collins, John M. *The Gliding Flight: Twenty Excellent Fold and Fly Paper Airplanes.* Berkeley, CA: Ten Speed Press, 1989.

Engel, Peter. *Folding the Universe: Origami from Angelfish to Zen.* New York: Vintage Books, 1989. (Also available as *Origami from Angelfish to Zen.* New York: Dover, 1994.)

Juster, Norton. *The Dot and the Line: A Romance in Lower Mathematics*. New York: Random House, 1963. (Paperback 1991.)

Morris, Campbell. *The Best Paper Aircraft*. New York: Perigee Books, 1986.

Robinson, Nick. *Paper Airplanes*. London: Quintet Publishing, 1991 (Secaucus, NJ: Chartwell Books, 1991).

The Visual Geometry Project. *The Platonic Solids Activity Book*. Berkeley, CA: Key Curriculum Press, 1991. (See also accompanying videotape below.)

Weiss, Stephen. *Wings & Things: Origami That Flies*. New York: St. Martin's Press, 1984.

Films and Videotapes

Donald in Mathmagic Land. Burbank, CA: Walt Disney Productions, 1959; Walt Disney Home Video, 1988.

The Dot and the Line: A Romance in Lower Mathematics. Hollywood, CA: MGM, 1965. (Academy Award winner.)

Flatland. New York: McGraw-Hill Films, 1965.

The Platonic Solids. Berkeley, CA: Key Curriculum Press, 1991.

Recordings

Songs of the Humpback Whale. Recorded by Roger S. Payne. Hollywood, CA: Capitol Records, 1970.

Deep Voices. Recorded by Roger S. Payne. Hollywood, CA: Capitol Records, 1977. (Also includes songs of blue and right whales.)

Origami Societies

These organizations publish newsletters and are valuable sources of all kinds of information on the art of paper folding. Include a stamped, self-addressed envelope when you write to them.

Origami USA
15 West 77th Street
New York, NY 10024-5192

British Origami Society
Penny Groom, Honorary Secretary
2A The Chestnuts
Countesthorpe
Leicester LE8 3TL
England

Further Exploration   *179*

Folding Hints

🐤 Paper usually folds best upon a flat, smooth surface.

🐤 Start with clean, dry hands, and allow yourself plenty of elbow room and plenty of time.

🐤 Be sure to line up the edges of your paper slowly and carefully before you start to crease it, and make your folds as crisp and accurate as you can. Airplane wings need to match perfectly for well-balanced flight.

🐤 You can find three-dimensional, interactive, step-by-step instructions for making your own Owl, Albatross, Manta Ray, Eagle, Condor, and Saturn planes in the "Greatest Paper Airplanes" computer software. And there are many excellent books about paper airplanes and other origami shapes, too.

🐤 Be sure to experiment with different types and sizes of paper. You will find that recycled photocopy paper is especially good for airplanes, as well as plain, lined notebook paper.

🖢 Folded paper may have sharp edges, though, so planes should never be aimed at people or animals.

🖢 Experiment with your finished plane. You may need to trim (or adjust the angles of) your airplane, and remember also that different designs need different throwing techniques: hard, soft, upward, downward. Some will fly outdoors; some won't.

🖢 Sometimes, too, a plane will fly better if you use a bit of tape or a paper clip or staple to hold it together, as well as to add weight. Paper helicopters in particular need to be weighted at the bottom. Try dropping them from different heights, using different amounts of weight, and see what happens.

🖢 Cups and boats made of coated paper are fairly waterproof.

🖢 Patterns for folding solid geometric shapes can be enlarged easily with a photocopy machine, and they may also be transferred or glued onto light cardboard for improved sturdiness.

🖢 And if you make your Möbius strip wide enough, you will be able to cut it in half (down the middle) several times in succession without ever cutting it in two!

Susan Lowell lives on a small ranch in southern Arizona at the base of Baboquivari, a mountain peak sacred to her neighbors, the Tohono O'odham Nation. The region is embedded with a rich mixture of Native American, Mexican, and Anglo culture and folklore—flying coyotes, lost treasures, Indian cowboys, rubies in the sand. Lowell's family has inhabited the area for generations. Family stories, some handed down from pioneer days, fascinate her, and, although Lowell has lived elsewhere, it is from her experience in the West that her books have grown.

Lowell's first novel for older children, *I Am Lavina Cumming* (Milkweed Editions, 1993), was named book of the year by the Mountains and Plains Booksellers' Association and was also a *Hungry Mind Review* 1994 Children's Book of Distinction. *Ganado Red* (Milkweed Editions, 1988) won the 1988 Milkweed Editions National Fiction Prize and was named one of the best books of the year by *Publishers Weekly*. *The Three Little Javelinas* (Northland, 1992), a children's picture book, won the 1994 Arizona Young Readers' Award, and in that same year Lowell was named Arizona Children's Author of the Year by the Arizona Library Association. She has written two other children's picture books, *The Tortoise and the Jackrabbit* (Northland, 1994) and *Little Red Cowboy Hat* (Henry Holt, 1996).

Born in Chihuahua, Mexico, and educated at Stanford and Princeton, Lowell is married to photographer Ross Humphreys. They have two daughters, Anna and Mary.

Designed by Will Powers.
Typeset in ITC Stone Serif and Stone Sans
by Stanton Publication Services, Inc.
Printed on acid-free 55-pound Glatfelter paper
by Edwards Brothers, Inc.

If you enjoyed this book, you will also want to read these other Milkweed novels:

Gildaen, The Heroic Adventures of a Most Unusual Rabbit
by Emilie Buchwald

Chicago Tribune Book Festival Award,
Best Book for Ages 9-12

Gildaen is befriended by a mysterious being who has lost his memory but not the ability to change shape at will. Together they accept the perilous task of thwarting the evil sorcerer, Grimald, in this tale of magic, villainy, and heroism.

The Summer of the Bonepile Monster
by Aileen Kilgore Henderson

Milkweed Prize for Children's Literature

Eleven-year-old Hollis Orr has been sent to spend the summer with Grancy, his father's grandmother, in rural Dolliver, Alabama, while his parents "work things out." As summer begins, Hollis encounters a road called Bonepile Hollow, barred by a gate and a real skull and bones mounted on a board. "Things that go down that road don't ever come back," he is told. Thus begins the mystery that plunges Hollis into real danger.

I Am Lavina Cumming
by Susan Lowell
Mountains & Plains Booksellers
Association Award

In 1905, ten-year-old Lavina is sent from her home on the Bosque Ranch in Arizona Territory to live with her aunt in the city of Santa Cruz, California. Armed with the Cumming family motto, "Courage," Lavina deals with a new school, homesickness, a very spoiled cousin, an earthquake, and a big decision about her future.

The Secret of the Ruby Ring
by Yvonne MacGrory
Winner of Ireland's
Bisto "Book of the Year" Award

Lucy gets a very special birthday present, a star ruby ring, from her grandmother and finds herself transported to Langley Castle in the Ireland of 1885. At first, she is intrigued by castle life, in which she is the lowliest servant, until she loses the ruby ring and her only way home.

A Bride for Anna's Papa
by Isabel R. Marvin
Milkweed Prize for Children's Literature

Life on Minnesota's iron range in 1907 is not easy for thirteen-year-old Anna Kallio. Her mother's death has left Anna to take care of the house, her young brother, and her father, a blacksmith in the dangerous iron mines. So she and her brother plot to find their father a new wife, even attempting to arrange a match with one of the "mail order" brides arriving from Finland.

Minnie
by Annie M.G. Schmidt

Winner of the Netherlands' Silver Pencil Prize
as One of the Best Books of the Year

Miss Minnie is a cat. Or rather, she was a cat. She is now a human, and she's not at all happy to be one. As Minnie tries to find and reverse the cause of her transformation, she brings her reporter friend, Mr. Tibbs, news from the cats' gossip hotline—including revealing information that one of the town's most prominent citizens is not the animal lover he appears to be.

Mission Statement

Milkweed Editions publishes with the intention of making a humane impact on society, in the belief that literature is a transformative art uniquely able to convey the essential experiences of the human heart and spirit.

To that end, Milkweed Editions publishes distinctive voices of literary merit in handsomely designed, visually dynamic books, exploring the ethical, cultural, and esthetic issues that free societies need continually to address. Milkweed Editions is a not-for-profit press.